My Immortal Cowboy

Hell's Cowboys Book 1

By: Victoria Zak

Copyright

My Immortal Cowboy, Hell's Cowboys Book 1

Victoria Zak

Copyright © Victoria Zak, 2016

Edited by: Violetta Rand and Julie Roberts

Cover by: JAB Designs

ISBN-13: 978-1942516125

Contents

Chapter One

The roar of the Sunday crowd was deafening as shouts of encouragement rang across the Horns and Spurs arena. RC Reid lowered himself down and straddled a fifteen-hundred-pound bull in the chute. He gripped the handle hold of the bull rope with his left hand, testing the tackiness of the rosin.

A cowboy working the pens leaned over the top of the metal fence. "Got him nice and tight?"

RC nodded.

"No rider wants to leave money on the table by losing his rope."

The beast charged forward as the bucking strap was set in place. There was good reason his ride was named Hell's Fury. He was wild in the chute and rode like he was dragging you to hell. It ignited the adrenaline surging through RC's veins. He liked 'em mean and aggressive. At the end of the dance, victory was that much sweeter.

Nothing was going to stop this up-and-coming cowboy star from riding this mean sonofabitch for eight seconds.

He'd ridden bulls all of his life. It was the only thing he knew, and right now he was at the top of his game and loving every second of it. Tonight was the last of a four-day event and he was the one to beat. Throughout the season he'd ridden through broken ribs, bone-deep bruises, and bloodshed, yet he always got back on his feet again, kicking the dirt off his boots, and dusting the arena grime from his Wranglers. There was no room for intimidation to rattle his concentration. Not even the preshow fireworks and loud music shook his nerves. His focus was on the ride.

He recalled standing in front of the flashing lights a few minutes ago, the crowd cheering his name. A woman he'd never seen before had walked past him, taking a seat in the front row, her striking blue eyes standing out against black-as-night hair so long it kissed her perfectly shaped ass. A white tank top hugged her curvy frame, exaggerating her full breasts. Skin-tight rhinestone jeans that sat low on her hips finished off the outfit. At first he'd brushed her off as just another buckle bunny, but when she tipped her Stetson and gave him a wicked smile, something shook his soul. The twinkle in her eyes sent out a warning instead of an invitation—he'd see her again.

Quickly, RC refocused on the monster between his legs. *Controlled and consistent.* The words he lived by looped inside his head as he pulled his hat down, securing the black felt for the ride. Taking in a deep breath, he tucked his chin to his chest. The time felt right. He was ready to slay the dragon and win tonight's prize money. If he did, he'd qualify for the Professional Bull Riders' World Championship in Las Vegas.

Once he'd set his sights on something, he'd never quit until he got what he wanted. Hardheaded? Nah, determined.

But the real prize if he won, was getting one step closer to starting his life with Charlee Brysen. He'd loved that girl from the moment he'd set eyes on her at the age of twelve. A memory flashed and he was back home, dangling his hook in the creek that ran between the Brysen's and his family's land, staring at Charlee as she cast her own line into the dark water.

He loved the way her cheeks flushed and her lips pressed together during those awkward moments when he'd been caught gawking. As they grew older, there was more to Charlee that set him on fire. He'd move heaven and earth to be with the blonde from Diablo, Texas again.

Gripping the top of the fence with his right hand, he pushed his hips forward, eyes still locked over the bull's shoulders. RC nodded and the gate opened, unleashing Hell's Fury. The bull bucked into the area, its hooves pounding into the ground, slinging dirt and spit in every direction. The bastard turned tight to the left, toward his riding hand, just the way he liked it. Adrenaline pumped through his veins full force as the crowd roared to life, encouraging him to ride the full eight seconds.

"RC Reid," the announcer yelled out in excitement, "is making history tonight, folks!"

As he chased his dream, he was confident and in control, until the bull threw his head back, knocking RC off balance. The force of the buck tossed his body forward and his head connected with one of the beast's horns. The arena turned into a rippling blur as he fought back the haze threatening to take over.

Worry crept in when his body became numb. As the battle spin continued, there was no stopping his body from falling into the vortex of dust, hooves, and bull spit. Fury kicked out his hind legs with such power that RC lost his grip and was thrown to the dirt.

The bull fighters rushed the massive animal, waving their hands in the air, trying desperately to distract him. Heavy hooves crashed down onto RC's chest before he had a chance to roll out of the way.

His lungs constricted and he gasped for air.

Second by second, the darkness beckoned him deeper into oblivion. Cowboys didn't walk away from bull wrecks like this. He'd seen his share and knew this ride was fatal, but before he went to his grave, he had to know if it'd been worth it.

Would he die knowing he had given that sonofabitch his all? He looked up at the time clock. Well, if this didn't put the pickle on the shit sandwich. Eight seconds—he'd ridden for eight seconds. He closed his eyes as he heard the paramedics rushing toward him.

RC lay in a broken heap in the arena. A series of sorrowful cries echoed from the bleachers. The enthusiastic tone from the announcers morphed to a grim silence when RC failed to stand and walk away from the wreck.

Voices became mere murmurs as questions were being fired his way. His lungs burned, the fight to stay alive fading fast. The iron taste of blood flooded his mouth. One of the first responders wrapped a brace around his neck. He swallowed hard. Was he really going out like this? Even though they tried to outrun it, every bull rider knew that death was a possibility.

He'd never get a chance to tell Charlee how much he'd sacrificed for their love. Now he cursed himself for breaking up with her two years ago. At the time he'd thought it best, so Charlee could focus on college without worrying about his dream. Even though he knew the split wasn't final, he'd never get the chance to tell her how truly sorry he was for letting her go.

As he lay there, a beautiful vision of Charlee flashed before him. She was sitting at their favorite fishing hole, the sun shining through the trees casting a warm glow across her skin, a smile on her face that made his stomach flop like a fish out of water. He'd never forget that smile. His chest tightened into a wad of knots as he thought about leaving her alone. She was the reason he'd endured the beatings and pushed through the heartache every damn night. He rode for their future. All he had to do was make it to the championship, claim the million-dollar prize, and go home with a nest egg big enough to live comfortably on.

Now he fought for his life.

It wasn't supposed to end like this.

His lungs begged for oxygen, but he lacked the strength to drag in a single breath. Voices traveled down a faraway tunnel, never reaching him as he lost consciousness.

RC gulped for air and opened his eyes wide. The buckle bunny that had been sitting in the front row was bent over him with her lips pressed to his, blowing life back into his body. When their eyes met, she lifted her head and smiled down at him, flashing her white teeth.

He coughed through his dry throat. "Who are you?" he asked, stunned to see her. "The fucking Death Angel?"

She laughed. "Darlin', I'm here to bring you home."

What? He surrendered to the darkness again.

Chapter Two

RC had no idea if he was alive or dead. All he knew was that every muscle in his body ached like he'd been beaten with a baseball bat. He moaned back to life as he gingerly rubbed his bandaged ribs, which pulsed with pain. Cold fingers swept across his forehead reminding him he wasn't alone. He clutched his stomach, groaning as he rolled into a tight ball, bracing himself against the internal torture.

"Darlin', don't fight it."

The familiar voice sent chills down his spine.

RC turned onto his back. Mumbled words swam through his mind and thumped to the beat of his aching head as he tried to shake off the fog. He opened his eyes, and a pair of ruby lips flashed into a smile.

"Hello, darlin'."

Shit! He was six feet under, and the devil—in the form of a buckle bunny—she'd come to take his soul straight to hell. It had been just his luck; death had sunk its icy claws into him when he wasn't ready to die.

"Selene, perhaps we should let him rest." Another woman, this one with blonde hair, stepped into view.

Selene shot her an irritated glare. "Thana, when I want your opinion, I'll ask for it."

The blonde shrugged her shoulders and retreated. Clearly the woman knew her place and it wasn't to question the buckle bunny's authority.

"Darlin', can you hear me?" Selene sat on the bed and ran her fingers though his hair.

He rubbed his jaw, wondering why it hurt like he'd just had a root canal on every damn tooth. Then again, he was in so much pain it was hard to tell where each ache ended and another one began. Whatever had happened, he wasn't in Texas anymore. He needed to get the hell out of there, wherever *there* was, but first he had to figure out who these women were.

Whoever they were, they weren't there to offer the typical romp buckle bunnies offered. They possessed a power he couldn't explain. It rolled off them in waves and sent his instincts into flight or fight mode. A strange vibration rushed through his veins and the same power he sensed in the women overtook him, giving him the strength he needed to fight, and hopefully the stamina to get to the flight part of his plan. With a speed that belied his pain, RC leapt on top of Selene, pinning her beneath his body, his hand on her throat before his brain had even processed the offensive move.

"Who are you and why am I here?"

"You're strong, Cowboy." She bit her bottom lip. "I like it rough."

"Selene," Thana warned.

"Oh, come on. Can't we have some fun?" She rolled her eyes as if the whole situation bored her.

Before he knew what had happened, Selene had him on his back, stripping away any control he'd thought he had. She held his wrists above his head with one hand, and cupped his prized goods with the other. "If you ever touch me like that again…these," she squeezed his balls, "will be mine."

He swallowed hard, stunned at the power packed behind this woman. She couldn't be more than a hundred pounds wet, yet he was powerless against her. For fuck's sake, he'd ridden fifteen-hundred-pound bulls for a living! *Who…no, more like what the hell is she?*

"Are you going to play nice?" she asked.

"It depends," he hissed through the pain as her grip tightened around his cock. "Only if you tell me where I am and who you are?"

She pinned him with a hard glare; her white teeth gleamed against the dark-lit room. Something in that expression told him that she never played fair *or* nice.

She relaxed her hold. "My name is Selene and this is Thana." She pointed to the blonde standing next to her. "We're here to help you."

He didn't believe her, but something sinful and familiar raced through his blood, the strange power sparking every nerve ending. He'd taken his last breath back at the arena, but why then did he feel more alive than ever?

"You can trust us," Thana added.

"Right. How can I trust you when I haven't a clue who you are? For all I know I'm in some kind of purgatory at the mercy of death angels." He sat up, rubbing the ache between his legs.

Selene chuckled. "Oh, I like that, Cowboy. The angel of *DEATH*."

Selene's eyes sparked with enthusiasm as she said the last word, making his skin prickle. Yep, something wicked was going on.

"We need to go." Thana tossed RC a shirt, then placed his boots by the bed.

"Not until you tell me what's going on." He shoved his arm through the sleeve of the plaid button-down and nearly ripped the shirt in two as he pulled it over his shoulder. "What the hell?"

"How cute, he doesn't know his own strength." Selene pinched his cheek.

He swatted her hand away. "Don't touch me."

"Selene, you know how Roman doesn't like to wait." The blonde walked toward the door. The sound of her boots scuffing along the floor echoed across the room.

"Fine," Selene huffed and stood. "Look, Cowboy, you're home now, and Roman will explain everything. Just trust us. We're not here to hurt you, that is if you play nice." She winked.

RC shoved his feet into his boots. He eyed Selene, then gazed at Thana, leery of their true intentions. Who was this Roman? If he was going to find the truth, he had to leave this room, and if it meant trusting these women, he'd play along, but on his own terms.

"All right, ladies, I'll go with you on one condition." He stood and smiled, giving Selene a heavy dose of his own charm. No woman could resist his boyish, make-you-go-weak-in-the-knees dimples and his southern charm.

Or so he thought.

In one fluid motion, Selene stood behind him, tightening a leather collar around his neck, and Thana had both his hands tied behind his back. They'd jumped him like they were roping a calf. Before RC could register what had just taken place, Selene pulled him forward by a leash attached to the front of the collar. He stumbled toward the door.

He tugged against the restraints. "What the hell!" Silver spikes pricked against his skin and burned him like hellfire.

Selene brushed her lips against his ear. "There are no conditions, Cowboy. Our way only." She gave the collar a tug.

Point taken.

"Please, don't try to fight," Thana whispered behind him. "You'll only make it worse."

"When I break free…" he threatened through clenched teeth, "I'll kill you both."

Selene laughed, pulling him down a dark hallway.

Bright sconces lined the walls and lit their way as they walked deeper into the tunnel. His eyes sensitive to the harsh glow, he blinked back the stinging tears and started to count the lights, memorizing every detail of his surroundings so when the right moment arrived, he'd know the way out of this hell.

There were no windows or doors; nothing but stone walls on either side of him. A dank, earthy smell invaded his senses, his gut telling him he was underground.

The hallway dead-ended, with nothing but a wall of rock in front of him. There was no way out, unless he backtracked twenty-two sconces. Then where would he go? For the first time in his life he'd found something that rattled his cage. He was trapped.

His vision went black. "What the…?" He fought against the restraints which only caused the collar around his neck to burn hotter.

"It will be over soon," Thana said as she tied a blindfold over his eyes.

RC tried to keep his mouth shut, but his patience was wearing thin and he was nearing his breaking point.

He heard what sounded like a door sliding open before he was pushed against a cold wall. He was defenseless. His heart jumped at the sound of a loud thump, followed by an unexpected jolt. He was thrown off balance as he felt the floor beneath him drop. Shit, was he in an elevator, and going down?

"He really needs to fix that," Thana huffed. "I swear to the Goddess if I get stuck in here—"

"I know. It's not like we haven't been complaining about this for months," Selene agreed.

Even with the unknown looming ahead of him, he found their complaints quite amusing. No matter what, women were women; always yappin' about something.

The elevator came to a sudden stop and RC could feel the women's bodies tense; could hear their blood flowing through their veins. He could hear saliva being swallowed in fear. Whoever they were going to see was bad news if these women were afraid.

He was yanked forward and this time he didn't protest. Something stirred inside him, something he hadn't felt before. Even though Selene and Thana were complete strangers, the urge to protect them overran all caution.

Instantly he was assaulted by the sweet, pungent smell of cigar smoke. *Where am I?* The blindfold was ripped from his face. His vision blurred back to life as his eyes adjusted to the bright room. A broad-shouldered man stood at the far end of the room, where another man wearing a cowboy hat sat with his booted feet propped on a desk. Intensity poured off the man in waves, sending out a warning RC heard loud and clear. Whoever this man was, he was in charge.

One thing was for certain; judging by the way the man rolled the head of his cigar across his lips as if he was kissing his lover, he obviously enjoyed a good smoke.

Squinting through the acrid haze, RC studied the room. The walls were cushioned in red leather, probably for soundproofing, which didn't bode well for him. Oak bookcases filled with leather-bound books lined the wall behind the desk. There were no windows. No natural light anywhere, which made RC want to run. Even though he had no weapons, he'd fight like hell when the shit went down, and judging by the looks of it, it was definitely going down.

Selene threw the torture collar and rope on the desk. "He doesn't care for the rope."

What the…? RC's hands flew to his neck, wondering when she'd removed his restraints.

"Russel Cage Reid," the man from behind the desk drawled. "Welcome home." He stood, removed his cowboy hat, and walked over to RC offering his hand in introduction. "Roman McCoy."

RC refused to shake.

"Well, this wasn't the warm reception I'd hoped for," Roman confessed.

RC's stomach turned. How did this man know his full name? There was only one person who ever got away with calling him Russel, and that was his Charlee.

Growing tired of all the secrets, RC struggled to control his anger. "I want to know what's going on, and I want to know now."

Roman acted as if he had all the time in the world as he studied the cowboy, infuriating RC even more. "Son, you're in no place to be barking orders."

"Show some respect," the broad-shouldered man growled out, breathing heavily through his nose.

RC glanced at the big man. Knowing he was outnumbered and outsized should have been enough to keep his damn mouth shut, but this whole situation sent him orbiting into pissed-the-hell-off space.

He looked back at Roman. "Really? You abducted me and I'm the one breaking the rules? In case you didn't hear me the first time, asshole, I want to know why I'm here."

Before he could blink, Roman was in his face; his hands fisted in his shirt collar, his nostrils flared and his hot breath poured over RC's skin. "Let's make this clear, son, I call the shots around here. Once you understand that, we'll get along just fine."

Roman flashed his teeth and RC swore he saw fangs.

"Now that we have that out of the way..." Roman fixed RC's shirt. "I'll tell you what I want you to know, when I want you to know it, and if you get out of line, Nash here will put you back in it." He nodded to the big man behind the desk who was cracking his knuckles with a little too much enthusiasm for RC's taste.

Roman crossed his arms over his chest. "Russel, there's a lot that you have been blind to. I apologize. Your maker should have better prepared you."

Selene leaned over and whispered something in Roman's ear. Roman turned his attention back to RC. "Excuse me. Your father should have prepared you better."

"My father died sixteen years ago."

Thana offered RC a shot of whiskey, but he waved her off.

"I'm going to hit you with the cold, hard truth, son. RC Reid died out there in the arena three days ago. My angel," he pointed at Selene, "brought you home and

15

nursed you back to health. You're no longer a human. You're *dhampir*."

RC froze and placed his hand over his heart. It was beating...racing, actually.

Roman took a pull from his cigar, then stared at the burning embers.

"Yes, I know what you're thinking," he said. "If I'm dead, then why is my heart still beating? You're half human and half vampire. You have all the benefits of being human. You can walk in the sunlight and eat meat if you so choose." Roman wrinkled his nose as if the thought alone gave him indigestion. "But your strengths and desires...your soul, is vampire. It's been inside you ever since you were born."

RC couldn't believe what he was hearing. It couldn't be true. Vampires didn't exist. "Is this a joke? Seriously, I'm not impressed."

"No, son, this isn't a joke." Selene handed Roman the Sunday special edition of the Diablo Tribune. "Here, read this."

"Congratulations, darlin', you made the front page," Selene drawled.

Bile rose in the back of his throat as he snatched the paper from Roman. *Holy Christ!*

Young Bull Rider Warrior's Last Ride...

Tragedy struck Sunday night at the Horns and Spurs Texas arena when the up-and-coming bull rider, RC Reid was fatally injured as he rode Hell's Fury for a full eight seconds. Dr. Banks told reporters that Mr. Reid was pronounced dead shortly after

16

arriving by ambulance at Diablo Medical Hospital Sunday evening, citing internal injuries after being trampled. Millions of fans watched the scene unfold during the live broadcast. "RC left his mark on the bull ridin' world and will never be forgotten," said longtime friend and fellow bull rider, Luke Michaels.

The newspaper slid from his hands. He snatched up the bottom of his button-down and tore off the bandages around his ribs. He rubbed his hands frantically over his chest and abdomen. No evidence of even a scratch. Even though he remembered the events that took place that night, he was still clinging onto a shred of hope that it had all been a dream; that he would wake up and walk out of the arena. Instead he was stuck inside this nightmare, cursing his luck. The burning sensation surging through his veins was like nothing he'd ever experienced before and he couldn't explain the sudden change in his strength. He ran his finger down one of his throbbing canines. It hadn't changed, but his upper jaw ached like he'd been punched in the face. *Could it be true?*

"Russel, do you remember a time throughout your life that you were ever sick? Does it strike you odd that you heal quickly and no scars remain?" Roman tapped out his cigar and walked back behind the desk.

RC paused as childhood memories flashed scene by scene. He was never sick, not even a sniffle. All the times he'd been kicked, thrown, and bitten training horses, injuries had never kept him down for long. He'd thought he was just a healthy kid, growing up on the farm. And yes, he healed quickly from bull riding wrecks, and his eyes were sensitive to the sun, but it never dawned on him that he was different from the other cowboys. Adrenaline masked the aches and pains, while the excitement of traveling to the next bull ride consumed all thought.

"Fact is, your father is a vampire and your mother is human. There's no changing that fate, son." Roman cleared his throat. "Think of it as a gift. Dhampirs are an extremely strong breed. You have all the benefits of a human...walking in the sunlight, though always protect your eyes from the sun. They'll light up like firecrackers on the Fourth of July once the sun comes up."

"But my soul is forever damned to hell." RC stuck Roman with a bitter stare.

"I can't change the past, Russel."

"My name is RC," he bit back. "I don't know who or what the hell you..." quickly he corrected himself, "y'all are." He pointed to Nash, then to Selene and Thana. "But I'm leaving." Tipping his hat, he nodded a goodbye.

"You can't go back."

The threatening tone of Roman's words stopped him in his tracks. He turned and faced him. "I don't care what that newspaper says. I didn't die. I'm here, breathing and alive enough to want to kick your ass, but smart enough to know when I'm outnumbered," he added when the man behind Roman tensed. "If I've been a damphir-vampire-whatever my whole life, then I'll go on being one just fine without you."

"You can't go back to your old life," Selene interrupted before he could turn to leave. "No mere human could have survived that bull wreck and you know it. If you go back, you put us all at risk. The humans can't know what you are."

The hiss of the elevator doors sliding open zipped through the room. A blast of cold air hit RC and he froze. Terror snaked down his spine. Everyone's demeanor in the room changed, and that alone spoke volumes, as in, one wrong move and his ass would be grass.

Slowly looking over his shoulder, three six-foot-plus, well-built cowboys stood like gods from the underworld staring him down. The one standing in front crossed his arms over his chest, his biceps bulging against the rolled up sleeves of his button-down shirt. They were dressed in blue jeans and steel-tipped boots that had done a lot of shit kickin', all three donning Stetsons that shadowed their faces.

One would think twice before messing with this lot.

A bright shine coming from the trio's belt buckles grabbed RC's attention. Matching silver skulls with blood-tinged fangs eerily glared back at him. Words were engraved around the skull, but were hard to make out. Wait…there were two words that stood out.

"Hell's Cowboys?" RC whispered.

Their intimidating stance filled the room as they stepped out of the elevator with long confident strides. The man leading the pack looked RC up and down as he passed by, chewing on a toothpick.

RC met his stare, never showing an ounce of fear. It took all his resolve not to ask the bastard what his problem was.

A strong slap on his back knocked RC forward, testing his balance. "That's right, sweet cheeks," a second man said as he walked past, flashing a wicked grin. The third said nothing.

"This is him?" the man with the toothpick drawled.

"Russel, this here is Clay Holiday," Roman began the introductions.

Clay leaned against the desk, folded his arms across his chest, and nodded, giving the impression he wasn't amused.

"This is Kit Garrett, and this one here is Tibbs Randall."

Tibbs stood with his feet apart and his hands on his hips. The bastard smiled the brightest, shit-eating grin and tipped his straw cowboy hat. "Howdy."

Two things RC had learned long ago: never let them see you sweat, and never mess with a bull, or you'll get its horns. Well, he was two-for-two, now. Even though he knew these men could beat him into next week, maybe even next year, he'd show no fear. If they were here to put a hurtin' on him, he'd take it like a man and ask questions later.

As RC sized the cowboys up, he planned his next move. "Roman, you still haven't told me *why* I'm here. It better be a damn good reason."

"Well, I'll be." Tibbs laughed. "Boys, we have a feisty stallion here." He cracked his knuckles.

"Stand down," Roman said. "He has every right to know why we called on him." Roman paused. "We need you. There's a world out there that won't make sense to you. But in time you'll adapt. Once I lived in peace with

20

my vampire coven, governing our people with respect and integrity. We welcomed your kind, because the fact remains, dhampirs are our children and we take care of our own. But not all of my coven brothers felt the same. They started a war against dhampirs and ordered all vampires to restrain from fathering anymore half-breed children. This did not set well with some of us, so we broke away from the corruption and went into hiding. It was the only way we could help our..." He paused as if he'd almost revealed something he should keep to himself. "Dhampirs."

RC stood silent. For a man who didn't believe in the supernatural, he was getting a quick history lesson and taking mental notes.

"The coven has made it perfectly clear. Anyone aiding a dhampir is considered a traitor and will be put to death. We've been in hiding for quite a long time, living like outlaws. Though I have many people guarding these tunnels, our brood is small."

"Then why do you need me?"

"First, it's only a matter of time before they find you, and you'll need our protection. Secondly, you've been recruited to train and become one of the underground's most feared and elite, a brotherhood of powerful dhampirs. Think of it as..." He snapped his fingers, "the Army. You'll train with the best." He nodded to Clay, Kit, and Tibbs. "You'll hone your vampire skills, and in two years, if you show promise, you'll earn your buckle and become one of Hell's Cowboys."

"So what, I sign my name on the dotted line and serve Hell for eight years like a good underground

21

solider?" He crossed his arms. "I appreciate the offer, but I decline."

"Son, this isn't Hell. There's no option here. You're in or you die. It's that simple."

RC glared at Roman, then to the trio standing in front of him. *Vampires?* Looked like he had no choice if he wanted to remain undead.

"Good." Roman said. "These boys will be your shadow for the next two years."

"Can't wait," RC bit back.

Clay scowled at RC. Removing the toothpick from his mouth, he took two long strides and stood eye-to-eye with the new recruit. "I'm going to have fun breaking that disrespectful mouth of yours."

RC scowled back, his nostrils flared.

Clay broke their stare-off first and walked to the elevator doors, the other two following in his wake. As Tibbs walked by, he pointed at the silver doors—*get your ass moving* implied. RC knew better than to fight; the battle was lost before it had begun.

"Wait," Roman called. "I almost forgot." He took the rope and threaded it through his hands until he reached the end. It was coiled to perfection. "Every Cowboy has a special, powerful weapon forged just for them. Since you enjoyed your leash so much, you'll be needing this." He tossed the rope to RC.

RC caught it and cursed under his breath. *Nice joke asshole*; he hated that rope. As he draped it over his shoulder, it started to glow. Tiny fibers woven into the threads lit up like a strand of white Christmas lights. *What the hell?*

"What's wrong, sweet cheeks? It's not like it's a snake. It won't bite ya."

RC shot a glance behind him at a snickering Tibbs.

Yeah, he'd better get used to being the butt of a long line of jokes—this guy was relentless.

The Cowboys piled into the elevator, and one jerky stop later, the doors slid open to a long corridor. Their heavy boot steps pounded a steady rhythmic march down the hallway. As they reached the end, Clay stopped in front of a door, a rusty five-pointed star mounted in the center. Without him touching the doorknob, the door swung open and Clay walked in like he owned the place.

RC entered, inspecting his surroundings. In the middle of the room, two white leather sectionals wrapped around a large black coffee table. The walls were painted in muted tans giving a fresh and clean, inviting feeling.

Tibbs wasted no time in making himself comfortable, falling into the cowhide couch and plopping his legs on the table—steel tips shining. "Home sweet home, sweet cheeks."

From out of nowhere, two white towels were launched at RC from Clay's direction. And wouldn't you know, they were billowy soft and smelled like an ocean breeze. Clay shoved a bottle of shampoo into his chest as he made his way to the couch.

"Get your damn feet off the table, Tibbs." Clay smacked his boot. "Maudeen will have your ass for dirtyin' her table." Sitting down opposite of Tibbs, Clay studied the new recruit. "Your room is on the right. You're bunking with him." He tipped his chin at the grinning bastard in front, the one wearing the straw hat.

RC glared his response.

"You'd better rest up," Clay warned. "Training starts at oh-four-hundred." His tone cautioned anyone who dared argue otherwise.

RC went along and kept quiet as he walked toward the bedroom door. With these cowboys as roommates, there was no chance of escaping—not tonight.

"Hey," Tibbs called. "My room is the door on the left."

"Got it."

"Oh, and if you need a little somethin', somethin'," Tibbs winked, "you know, to help you relax. There's a stack of Hillbilly Delights under my bed."

At that moment, Kit entered the room and threw a pillow at Tibbs, smacking him in the back of the head. "Is that all you think about?" asked Kit.

"Fuck you, you're just jealous," Tibbs shot back.

"Seriously, I've seen the type of bunnies you attract." He sat down next to Clay, crossing one leg over the other. "It's a good thing we're immune to human diseases or you'd have things antibiotics couldn't cure."

Tibbs shot him an eat-shit-and-die smirk.

The obnoxious bantering intensified RC's headache. He needed somewhere quiet to absorb all this shit. Shaking his head, he opened the bedroom door and walked into another room, which opened up like a fancy hotel suite. He found a shared living area that held two brown leather couches arranged in front of a state-of-the-art media center. Dark wood beams lined the ceiling and large flat gray stones covered the walls.

There was a different odor in the room. A mixture of pine and—yep, saddle soap. He picked up the jar of soap from the coffee table, then noticed a saddle perched on a stand next to a chair. Running his fingers over the horn, he hoped he'd get to ride again someday soon.

Putting the jar back, he saw two black doors behind the couches on opposite sides of the room. Between the doors, a framed picture of the same image he saw on their belt buckles stared back at him. What disturbed him the most was the blood dripping from the skull's fangs. He ran his finger down his canine—another reminder of what he was born to be.

"Room on the right," he reminded himself. So, he picked the door to the left.

If he was going to be within spitting distance of Tibbs, he needed to know a little more about him. RC cracked open the door and turned on the lights. A strong whiff of pine penetrated his senses. For fuck's sake, the room looked like a frat house. Video game controllers lay next to a big screen TV. A poster with a naked blonde holding her tits occupied the wall above the bed. Tipped-over beer bottles were stashed on his night stand with a tube of lube within grabbing distance.

"You've got to be kidding me." RC shook his head at a Hillbilly Delight magazine peeking out from under his bed. "I'm rooming with a man-child." RC shut the door

25

and pledged to never, and he meant never, enter frat boy territory again.

Before he entered his room, RC rested his head on the door and prayed that it would be clean. After witnessing the horror of the last one, God only knew what he was walking into. He opened the door and was pleasantly surprised. *Thank God!* Right out of one of those vacation brochures advertising their five-star, upscale hotel suites, the space was too fancy for his blood.

A black, four-poster king-sized bed took up a quarter of the area. One wall was lined with mirrors. Looking up at the ceiling, he noticed a rectangle of golden glass cubes casting a warm glow over the whole bedroom like rays of sunlight shining down. However, he knew the sun didn't shine in places like this.

He placed the towels on the bed, then made his way into the bathroom checking out the accommodations. The theme of black and warm gold carried through. And again, everything from the multi-spray shower to the huge black marbled garden tub and toilet, was high-end.

He sat on the bed, resting his elbows on his knees and his head in his hands, his jaw still throbbing. *Where to start?* The nightmare wasn't ending soon, in fact, it had only just begun.

Thinking back to what Roman had said about him never being sick and healing fast… He'd known early on that he was different, but how different…he never expected half human, half vampire.

Vampire blood raced through his veins and burned like flowing hot lava. All five senses were enhanced. He tasted the pine in the air, could feel the slightest vibrations, and he could hear the Cowboys' heartbeats coming from the next room. His brain was going to explode from stimulus overload. Something animalistic shifted inside him.

Frustrated, he sighed and ran his hands through his thick dark hair, then fell back into the bed. He'd never be the same again.

Questions and thoughts shot from one scene to another as he tried to make sense of this mess. *Dad is a vampire?* The last memory he had of the man was when he was five years old. His father had tucked him in for the night, then sat on the edge of the bed and said something he'd never forget; *"Son, your life here on Earth is nothing more than a blink of an eye. The afterlife is when your true life begins."*

He could still hear that deep southern drawl. It was the last time he saw his dad. Maw said that he'd been hit by a drunk driver on his way to bull ride in Oklahoma. Strange thing was she'd never mentioned him again after their talk. No tears, no funeral. As an only child, he grew up quick as his mother drowned her sorrows in the bottle.

Now none of that made sense. Was he truly dead, or alive and staying out of his life? Should he be out searching for him? Nah, the bloodsucker would be able to find him easy enough if he wanted to. For all he cared, his father had gotten his stake through the heart years ago and wasn't coming back.

Damn him for not telling the truth; the bastard had to have known. Damn him for leaving his maw. He tamped down his daddy issues, but then Charlee crept into his thoughts—the one person who could bring him to his knees.

It wasn't supposed to end like this. As he stared up into the glowing ceiling, images of Charlee rushed over him. Having so much to say and never knowing what might have been, crushed him. Charlee would never know how much he loved her or how much he missed her. Or would she? Could he stay away from her? Either way, it didn't matter—he was dead to her.

"Shit." He closed his eyes. Fate was a bitch.

Chapter Three

Two years later

Dolls and Devils Gentlemen's Club

Diablo, Texas

Charlee Brysen slammed the door of her beat up Chevy truck—her grandmother's hand-me-down. The rain pelted as she opened her umbrella. Because of the downpour and stalling out at the last intersection, she was already an hour late. Running to the back door of the D&D, on nights like this she wished it was her truck being valet parked and that she was entering the posh covered entrance instead of dodging puddles in the back.

The club was marketed as classy, appealing to wealthy men who paid well. Classy? That was debatable. This place catered to all types of demons and preyed on the weak. Whether drugs, fetishes, or alcohol, D&D catered to unquenchable desires and served its patrons well. That was what kept the doors open. Souls be damned.

To an insider who saw what went down in those dark, cozy nooks and corners, Charlee knew firsthand how *high-class* those men were. For the right amount of cash, anything goes.

Yet she refused to tarnish her soul. This stripping arrangement was temporary. Down on her luck two years ago, she'd stopped by the club to grab an application. She was relieved to see some of the dancers wearing masks. It was perfect. She could conceal her identity.

Inexperienced, her innocence had been glaring the day she'd auditioned for Val, the club owner, and Delilah, the den mother. She shook her head, remembering her first striptease and how many times she'd tripped and wobbled in her stilettos. When Delilah called the next day to say she'd got the job, Charlee had been shocked.

However, she grew more confident over the months. The pasties didn't bother her as much now. Lap dances were a different story. Even though that was where the money was, she seldom did one. Unable to get over being so close and personal with men she didn't know, she relied on tips from the stage the most.

After RC's death, the idea of grinding on a stranger just felt wrong.

Charlee opened the back door and entered the building, giving her umbrella a good shake before she closed it, and tossed it into a bucket. After removing her raincoat and hanging it to dry, she hustled down a hallway lined with framed pictures of celebrities who had visited the club since its opening night ten years ago. Running her fingers through her wet blonde hair, she hoped she'd have time to take a blow dryer to the mess of waves before she went on stage.

She entered the dressing room like a tornado, apologizing profusely to the other dancers. "I'm so sorry I'm late."

She rushed to her locker and shoved her purse on the top shelf, then removed her pink tee and grey yoga pants.

"No worries, hon. Jackie took your spot. You're on in thirty." The redhead returned her focus to the gold-framed mirror surrounded by bright lights, freshening her makeup.

"Thanks, Gia. The weather is horrible out there." Charlee tossed her bra into the locker and slipped into a black spandex vest with a plunging neckline, snapping the buttons in place.

"From what I've heard, it's supposed to rain all weekend," Gia said.

"Wonderful. I'm working all weekend." Charlee huffed as she pulled on hot shorts over her thong. "I should buy a boat so I can make it to work on time."

They both chuckled.

As Charlee organized her makeup on the counter, she looked up at a photo hanging on her vanity and froze. It was one of RC winning his first belt buckle. She sat down. *God, why does it have to hurt so bad?*

It had been two years since she said goodbye and he still haunted her. She'd reluctantly given him the break in their relationship that he'd asked for, but she'd never thought he'd leave her for good before they had a chance to work things out. She never understood his reasons, but had given him his space anyway.

At least it wasn't another woman; it was that damn old rodeo—bull riding fever had won his heart. She

31

looked at herself in the mirror. *If RC could see me now.* She shook her head, disgusted by her reflection.

If the stars had aligned, all she'd needed was two years, then she would have had a business degree, and could have opened the bakery she'd always wanted, keeping her grandmother's ranch from foreclosure. But fate always had a way of kicking her in the ass.

What would Gran think?

Her grandmother would be disappointed that she hadn't gone back to school. When she came home from college to go to RC's funeral, she hadn't expected to be hit by the news that Gran was ill. She couldn't leave knowing that she might not ever see her again. It had been her and Gran on their own since she was young. She owed her so much.

Charlee applied blush to her cheeks, thinking back on simpler times when Pop Pop would be out mowing the fields on his tractor. He'd call her over and put her on his lap to take the wheel while he sat behind her drinking a beer. It was devastating that Pop Pop had died when she was ten.

But those bittersweet memories kept her going. Even stripping couldn't pay all the bills at the ranch now. What she brought home barely kept the vultures at bay. Whatever had to be done she'd do it to keep her home— it was all she had now that RC was gone.

Can't wasn't in her vocabulary. Gran had raised a strong, confident granddaughter and fate had raised an independent woman, grabbing life by the balls and demanding to make it better.

Picking up the black lace mask she wore every night, she adjusted it so it fit perfectly around her eyes. She scrunched her hair into place, then took a step back. Pleased with the result, she smiled. Yep, she was in control again.

Jackie busted in from the stage like a dust devil whirling through the plains. Small and compact, she was packing a punch. "Where's Val?" she demanded, slamming her fuzzy pink handcuffs on the vanity, and wiping the sweat from her tan skin.

"What happened, Jackie?" Charlee asked.

"It's not *what* happened, but what's goin' to happen if that mother fucker doesn't bump up security." Jackie stomped over to her locker and threw her stilettoes inside. "Those bastards out there can't keep their hands to themselves. I spent half my time slappin' their grimy paws off me." She slammed the locker door and stormed out the back.

Charlee was so caught up in Jackie's dilemma she jumped when Val entered the dressing room.

"Val, honey," Gia purred. "You better not let J catch you, she's high on a bitch rage and you're the fuel to the fire." The redhead rolled her eyes.

"Mmmm, I love me some hot cocoa," Val smiled. "Texas, you're up." He pointed at Charlee.

The electrifying guitar riff cut through the dressing room, cueing her that she was on. The bass thumped an ass-shaking beat. She grinned. This was *her* song; a song that turned the club buck wild. Add a half-naked blonde shaking her money maker; she'd have the crowd eating from the palm of her hand. She'd dance her ass off to *The McLendon Brothers, Let Me Be the Shimmy to Your Shake.* Big money tonight.

Charlee adjusted her black Stetson, the silver sheriff star twinkling beneath the lights. *There's a new sheriff in town tonight.* Tipping her hat and giving herself a wink in the mirror, she grabbed her prop, a water pistol full of whiskey. *This will cool them down.*

Chapter Four

RC punched the small speed bag, alternating his fists rapidly, driven by aggression. Sweat poured down his broad back, drenching the waistband of his workout shorts. Like clockwork, he hit the Hell's Cowboys gym right after Clay's rigorous training drills.

The cowboy showed no mercy and demanded loyalty and complete discipline. In the two years he'd spent in the underworld, the Cowboys had trained him in all aspects of combat, including weapons, emergency response, the lay of the underground city tunnels which were dangerous and unpredictable, and most of all, knowing his enemy inside and out.

He'd gotten to know each Cowboy well, but nothing compared to Kit's realm.

A man of few words, Kit was a genius when it came to cyber technology. Located in a top secret area, the cowboy sat behind multiple computer screens like he was the commander of a spaceship sending out orders from the central control room.

There were surveillance monitors connected to cameras that were placed throughout the city, watching their enemies' every move. RC would bet it all on red that the cowboy could hack into Diablo City Stock Exchange with no problem. The man was the Central Intelligence Agency wrapped in Wrangler jeans and a black Stetson.

RC continued to take his anger out on the punching bag. Even after two years, he still resented his fate. He kept his word and trained hard, yet he wasn't any closer to becoming one of Hell's Cowboys and the freedom he craved. In the eyes of the others, he was still a rookie and wasn't fully trusted. He hit the bag harder and harder. He missed the sunlight, the green grass—his horses. And every damn night he missed Charlee.

The training had been brutal, but the physical changes were just as ruthless. He had powerful strength that he was still learning to control. The throbbing in his upper jaw had intensified, until his canines turned into sharp fangs that only elongated when he was aroused. No one had warned him of this small detail. He found out the hard way when Charlee crept into his dreams and he woke up with his dick as hard as a rock, and fangs.

"Hey!"

It was Tibbs, he could hear that mother fucker's boots stomping from a mile away. He kept boxing, ignoring him.

"Hey!" Tibbs yelled louder. When RC didn't respond, Tibbs grabbed the bag, popping it.

"What the fuck?" RC shot him a cold glare.

"Hold up," Tibbs said. "We're going topside tonight."

RC walked off the fatigue, catching his breath. "Topside?"

36

"Yep." Tibbs threw a towel at him. "Get showered, you stink."

RC wiped his face. "Where are we going?"

Tibbs flashed his pearly whites. "You'll see, sweet cheeks." As Tibbs turned to go, he added, "By the way, we're leaving in an hour."

The door slammed behind Tibbs.

Flinging the towel over his shoulder, RC headed for the showers.

Forty-five minutes later, the four cowboys stepped off the elevator and into a parking garage. He hadn't been topside since Selene brought him to the compound. Quite frankly, it felt refreshing knowing he'd soon be breathing the night air.

Clay lead them over to a Ram 3500 truck and unlocked the doors.

"Shotgun!" Tibbs called out, then slid into the passenger seat.

RC and Kit took their places in the back. Clay turned the key and the engine roared to life. RC could almost see a smile on Clay's face as he backed the truck out. The up-ramp they were on led to another tunnel and dead-ended at a double garage door. Clay reached over Tibb's lap and opened the glove compartment, pushing a button on a remote inside. The door lifted to pounding rain and a washed-out gravel road.

RC looked behind him and watched the door camouflage into the side of the mountain like it had never existed. He turned back around. "So, where are we going tonight?"

Tibbs grinned. "It's a surprise."

"Tibbs needs to get his rocks off," Clay said as he turned left onto the highway.

"Maybe you wouldn't be such a dick if you got laid every once in a while," Tibbs said sarcastically.

RC shook his head at Clay and Tibbs's love/hate relationship. Total opposites in the personality spectrum, they fought like a married couple. It was only a matter of time until fists started to fly.

"Did anyone remind the rookie to lock 'n' load?" Clay asked, changing the subject.

"Shit," Kit whispered under his breath.

"The rookie has a name and yes, I'm packin'."

Clay slammed his palm on the wheel. "I swear I must speak another language." He huffed. "What's the one rule we never break?"

"Always have a weapon on you. I know the rules, Clay. I have two pistols. I'm good," RC reassured him.

"No," Clay disagreed. "You're not good. Where's your rope?"

RC paused, realizing he hadn't thought about it. He'd been attached to that damn thing like a second skin. Taking the night off from it didn't seem like a big deal. "I didn't think I needed it. What's the big deal?"

Tibbs turned around. "You gotta keep your weapon on you at all times. Especially when going topside. The undead are everywhere and they play by their own rules. That's why we train so hard with our special weapons. These guns will only weaken those bloodsuckers. But your personal weapon will kill 'em." He reached under the seat. "Here, load your guns with this ammo. They're silver bullets designed to blow the suckers' heads off."

RC grabbed the box of bullets and loaded his pistols, pissed off. Having his balls busted on a regular basis was getting old. He'd let it slide—for now.

Clay pulled into a parking lot, slushing through the puddles, careful not to splash mud on his truck. He ignored the valet trying to flag him down. "They ain't touching my truck." He parked sideways, taking up three spaces.

"You're such a dick, man," Tibbs said as he opened the door.

"Yep," Clay agreed, getting out.

They made a run for the covered entrance of the club. Tibbs removed his cowboy hat and shook his head like a wet dog. "You could have parked closer. It's raining."

"Don't worry. You won't melt." Clay walked past him and into the club.

RC removed his hat too, shaking off the rain. He inhaled deeply, taking in the damp night air. God, he'd forgotten the clean smell of rain and how refreshing it felt on his skin. There was something about being topside that made him feel free. It made him think about all the little things he'd taken for granted.

From the corner of his eye, the big neon sign caught his attention. "Dolls and Devils Gentlemen's Club." *A strip club?*

RC eyed two bouncers standing by the club door checking identifications. These guys were built like a brick shithouse. One of the burly twins waved Clay through like the Cowboys were regulars. The music thumped in his chest as he entered the club, his eyes adjusting to the purple glow in the room.

A mixed crowd occupied the tables in front of a sparkling raised platform. A stunning woman was wrapped around the pole at center stage, giving the crowd a show. The cocktail waitresses were dressed to kill in form-fitting silver jackets that showed off their best assets. Their matching shorts showed just enough cheek to keep the patrons deep in the bottle. He had to admit this club was high on the hog; the classiest one he'd ever been in. And he'd seen his share traveling the rodeo circuit.

The D&D had a full house tonight which left him on alert. The smell of booze, sex, and cigars mixed together was a wild concoction, driving his senses into overdrive. With liquor flowing freely, he'd bet the farm a fight would break out at any time. What was it that Clay had branded into his brain? *Always expect the unexpected.* No doubt he'd be tested tonight.

Tibbs clasped his shoulder, breaking his thoughts. "Do a shot with me."

RC hadn't had a drink since he began training. What the hell, he deserved a little celebration. "Lead the way, big man."

RC followed Tibbs to the bar, while Clay and Kit found a table by the stage. In no time Tibbs was greeted by a lively filly who took their drink orders.

"Tequila. Two," Tibbs ordered.

RC faced the stage, watching a group of men pawing at a dancer and wondered what her story was. Why would any woman put up with that shit?

"Thanks, darlin'." Tibbs smiled at the bartender and handed RC a shot of whiskey. "Here's to nipples." They clinked glasses. "Without them, tits would be pointless." Tibbs grinned and threw back the shot, then slammed the glass on the bar. He ordered another round.

RC choked on Tibbs' attempt at a toast. "I don't know where you come up with this shit, man." He wiped his mouth with the back of his hand.

Tibbs leaned against the bar. "Listen, I need to tell you somethin'." Tibbs was never serious.

"Clay didn't want to make a big deal of it, but I feel differently. Tonight is your night, my friend. You've made it through the most intensive, ass-kickin' training anyone has ever had to endure. I won't lie—we put you through hell." Tibbs handed him another drink. "So, tonight, you're an official graduate." Tibbs lowered his voice and leaned into RC. "Not a Hell's Cowboy. You have to earn that buckle," he said. With a shot glass in hand, Tibbs pointed at the dancers. "This is your oasis tonight. Now go get laid!"

The man was something else. RC turned back to the bartender and motioned for another drink. As he waited, he wondered when the Cowboys were going to acknowledge his accomplishment. Not that he wanted to make a big deal out of it. A few nice words would have suited him just fine. Two years was a long time to have your ass rode hard, but now he was ready for the next step.

The lights dimmed and the DJ tapped the mic. The crowd grew quiet as he introduced the next dancer. "Are y'all on your best behavior?" The crowd roared. "There's a new sheriff in town and she's kickin' ass and takin' names! Are you ready for some shimmy shakin', Texxxasss!"

A man next to RC bumped his arm in a drunken attempt to clap his hands, spilling his drink. "Hey, watch it." He pushed back.

"Dang, man, you gots to see this." The man pointed to the stage, then cupped his hand around his mouth and hollered.

Pissed at his now wet sleeve, RC turned around, glancing at the stage. He lost his breath and his heart banged against his ribcage as the feisty dancer took the stage with water pistols, taming the howling and snapping wolves at her heels. *Hot damn! Shotgun Sally!*

His gaze traveled down her body and locked onto her hips as they swayed and pulled him in like some kind of voodoo spell. Something in the air drew him to her and he needed a closer look.

Finishing what was left of his drink, he left the bar and made his way to the stage. He shouldered past the dense crowd until he reached a better view. This woman was something else; her body lit up the stage. Long lean legs, full breasts, and an ass shake that knocked him over.

He couldn't take his eyes off her; she mesmerized him body and soul.

A trail of sweat ran down his cheek as his attention was drawn to her tits, bouncing from the top of her vest. He wanted to plant his face between them and squeeze them tight. Holy hell, the things he wanted to do to her. His cock strained against his Wranglers just thinking about her. *What the fuck, RC, get it together.*

Stalking the dancer like she was prey, he crept in closer, until nothing stood between him and the seductive sheriff. She wrapped her hands around the pole…good God, she licked her lips and he about fell to the floor. *Fuck me! Two years is too long without sex.*

It was bad enough that the sheriff costume piqued his interest, but the black lace mask really stirred him up. There was something erotic about not seeing her face. She flipped her hair and dipped down. *Christ!* His temperature rose to another level and he swore he heard the angels singing. He watched her slowly unbutton her top and all he could think about was how he wanted her to cuff him. He'd been a very bad boy.

The music slowed and so did Texas. RC sucked in a breath, anticipating her next move. Texas sensually turned away from the crowd and then looked over her shoulder, biting her bottom lip and teasing the boys in the front row. Her captivating grin sent a jolt of electricity straight to his cock. *Fuck!* She slid her hands down her body, then slowly bent over.

Suddenly the music picked up again and Texas ripped off her shorts, shaking that tiny ass. *Hellfire!* His pupils dilated, feeling his vampire side honing in on her

43

finest asset, ready to claim it, until a freckle on her left cheek tamed the urge. He did a double take. What the hell? He knew that ass!

The hair on the back of his neck bristled. A cloud of crimson fogged his vision. His ears rang. Everything around him swirled in slow motion like a funnel cloud. *What the fuck was Charlee doing here? Naked?*

It took him a few minutes to regain what control he had left. If he acted now, he'd snap. He'd run right up on stage, throw Charlee over his shoulder, and put some clothes on her after he tanned her hide. This wasn't her. His jaw ticked as he thought about how deeply she could be involved in this lifestyle. Charlee was a good girl. No…no…no. He shook his head, refusing to go there.

He felt a tap on his shoulder. "Can I get you something, sugar?" a cocktail waitress asked, licking her red lips.

"Yes," he said before he could stop himself. But the truth was he did indeed want something—a blonde wearing a black Stetson and stilettos. His heart took a nosedive straight into his stomach when reality hit him. Charlee thought he was dead; she'd freak if she saw him. And why wasn't Charlee away at college? Did Gran know what she was up to? The stars were not aligned here.

"I want her." He pointed to the stage.

"You mean Texas?" She looked at the stage. "You want a lap dance?"

"Yeah." He slipped her a five-hundred-dollar bill.

The waitress tucked it inside her low-cut vest. "I'll try my best, darlin'. But Texas doesn't do private dances."

"She does now." RC slipped her another five hundred. "I'll be waiting upstairs."

The waitress shrugged. "It's your money."

He wouldn't take no for an answer. "You make damn sure to tell *Texas* not to keep me waiting."

Chapter Five

"What?" Charlee buttoned up her vest.

"That's what he said." The waitress handed her the money.

"And you told him I don't do lap dances?"

"Yes. With this kind of money being thrown around, he's not going to take no for an answer."

Charlee slipped back into her shorts. With bills piling up, a thousand dollars was a lot to give up. She'd never been offered that kind of money for a lap dance.

"If it helps, the cowboy is drop dead sexy. Seriously, he's the type you'll want to be naughty with." The waitress winked.

Charlee rolled her eyes. A part of her was intrigued. She stood with her hands on her hips, skimming through the reasons not to give in. It was against her rules, yet she was curious. He wasn't a regular, because they all knew she was off limits. The cowboy was demanding and obviously rich. If he was willing to throw his money around, perhaps she should be willing to take it. She needed a rich man to take away all her troubles. Bathe her in designer clothes and diamonds. Make the mortgage payments on the ranch. Pay off Gran's medical bills. She laughed. Oh, who was she fooling? The cowboy wanted a piece of ass. She wasn't the pretty princess, and Prince Charming didn't hang out at titty bars.

She fisted the bills in her hand. "Which booth did he say he'd be in?"

The waitress grinned. "Second booth in V.I.P."

Charlee put her Stetson on. Curiosity was a bitch. She had to see this cowboy. "Thanks."

She sashayed up the stairs to the V.I.P. level where it opened to a loft. Couches sectioned off small gathering areas where men and women sat drinking and flirting. A strange electricity tinged with sex, sweat, and alcohol lingered. Cold air prickled her skin as she made her way to the private rooms. She glanced at a couple in the corner, making out hot and heavy. The woman leaned her head back while the man kissed up and down her neck and fondled her breasts. The man lifted his head and smirked wickedly at her. She blushed from being caught gawking, and was hit with surprise when he motioned for her to join in. Quickly, she averted her gaze and picked up the pace, hightailing it out of his sight. God, she hated coming up here. Hungry eyes looked at her from all directions, undressing her straight through to her soul. She felt like a little lamb being thrown to the lions. Fortunately for her, in the last two years, she'd only visited this area a handful of times.

"T, what are you doing up here?" A tall well-built man stood from a comfy corner chair.

Charlee knew that deep tone and relaxed. Thank God it was Vin. "Hey." She stopped and hugged him.

"It's not like you to be up in V.I.P. What's going on?" Vin was Val's twin brother and the more approachable one. From day one they'd connected and he quickly became the big brother she'd never had. He protected her, and she trusted him with her life.

"I'm fine."

Vin folded his arms across his chest and eyed her up and down suspiciously.

"Just need to make some extra cash. That's all." She shrugged her shoulders.

"Is the guy a regular?"

"I don't know for sure, but probably not."

"I got your back, T." Vin's smile was all she needed to calm her rattled nerves, and added to that was the fact that he was packing and carried a big fuck-off stick.

A few seconds later she was standing outside the booth where she knew the cowboy waited. Was she actually going to go through with it? Do a lap dance? Blowing out a breath, she made sure her mask was secure.

She pushed open the curtains, then stepped inside. Her heart jumped. This wasn't what she had expected. She was caught off guard by the sexy cowboy sitting leisurely with his legs wide open and his arms resting over the back of the booth; the room reeked of raw male testosterone.

His face was shadowed under the brim of his black cowboy hat, except for his closely-shaven jaw. Her gaze moved to the crisp, white button down, then to his silver belt buckle and crotch-hugging Wranglers, which she had to admit, showcased his…package quite nicely.

"What took you so long?" he asked.

Charlee couldn't miss the full lips that were apparently talking to her. Sweat beaded on her forehead. *When did it get so hot?*

She cleared her throat. "I-I wasn't sure I should come."

"Well, I'm glad you did."

There was a hidden demand to his deep, rich tone that made her heart pound. And the tingle between her legs… No one did that to her. Only RC, and he was gone forever. "Why did you demand to see me? There's plenty of girls around here willing to give you what you want."

"I chose *you.*"

For some reason, hearing him say that made her go weak in the knees.

The cowboy shifted in his seat and leaned forward. "You're not willing?"

"No. I don't give lap dances." Charlee placed her hands on her hips, ready for the cowboy's temper to catch up to his libido. It always did. Every cowboy she'd ever known had one and he'd show his eventually.

"Is that so, *sheriff?*"

Charlee eyed him from his hat to his boots. "Looks like we have a problem."

A wicked grin spread across his lips. "Are you scared? I don't bite. Hard."

"Scared?" She smirked. "No. And you'll never know how it feels to bite me because this conversation is over." She turned to leave.

"Well, darlin', if you can't handle being with a *real* cowboy—"

She didn't like being called a coward. Even though he hadn't said it directly, she knew what he meant. Striding back to his chair, she placed her stilettoed foot between his legs, ready to stomp his balls. She tipped his chin upward to get a good look at his face, but his hat still shielded her view. "Darlin'," she mocked. "I can handle anything that comes my way, even a cocky sonofabitch like yourself."

When he smiled, Charlee did a double take. She knew that dimple. "Take off your hat."

"Oh, you won't give me a lap dance, yet you want me to take off my hat." He ducked out of reach as she went for his Stetson.

Before she had a chance to try again, he scooped her into his lap. Involuntarily straddling him, she pushed on his chest to get away. "If you don't let me go, I'll scream. Vin is right outside."

"I don't want to hurt you. If you promise to put down your guns, I'll let you go."

She agreed and he let go of her hips.

His hands sliding up her thighs should have been reason enough to make her call for Vin, but his touch was familiar—almost comforting. He continued to caress her arms, then lightly touched her neck, stopping at her cheek. She closed her eyes, nuzzling into his hand as he cupped her face. Yes, she knew that touch. Craved it every day. Each tender stroke left her wanting more.

When he removed her mask she gasped, feeling helpless.

"By God, Charlee girl, I've missed you." Then he revealed his own face, dropping his hat on the table.

Surprised that he knew her name, Charlee met his gaze. That face… Those eyes… His cocky expression… All too real. Her heart ached from the memories. The pain of losing him.

"No, no, no." She bolted off his lap and backed away until she hit the wall behind her. "I went to your funeral. This isn't possible." She closed her eyes. What the fuck was going on? Was she dreaming? Going crazy? If she opened her eyes would the cowboy still be there? A dead ringer for RC … a freak of nature, nothing more. Didn't experts say everyone had a twin in the world?

"Charlee, I can explain everything. You have to trust me."

Cautiously, she opened her eyes. Their gazes locked as he stood and approached with his hands raised in surrender.

"I won't hurt you," he said tenderly, standing in front of her.

"You can't be alive." Tears streamed down her face. "You just can't…"

"Darlin'." He took her hand and placed it over his heart. "I'm flesh and bone."

The pain on his face told her the truth. This was no stranger.

She felt his steady heartbeat and the heat radiating off his muscular body. Confusion, shock, and relief collided inside her as adrenaline took over. For a moment she stared at him like he was a ghost, waiting for him to disappear. It didn't make sense. But...

Anger took over. She made a fist and slugged him in the face. RC stumbled back. "How dare you die on me, Russel Cage!" She pounded his chest relentlessly, letting out all the rage and pain that had built up inside. "You left me!" His refusal to react made her angrier. "Say something!"

He rubbed his jaw. "Nice right hook, woman."

A moment of silence passed between them and then she chuckled, palming the tears away. "Is it really you, RC?"

She looked up at him, needing to be certain.

"Yeah."

She nodded, accepting what she still couldn't explain and wrapped her arms around his neck, holding on tight. She'd never let him go again.

"I'll explain everything once—"

Rapid gunfire rang out as two men rushed into the room. RC pulled her to a corner behind the booth. "What's going on?"

"Stay down!"

Charlee huddled into a ball, covering her ears while RC fired back, hitting one of the gunmen.

RC motioned for Charlee to stay quiet as the remaining attacker approached the booth, broken glass crunching beneath his feet. Her heart raced as RC shot up from behind the bench and fired.

RC crept out, pointing his semi-automatic left, then right—all was clear. Booting one of the dead lying on the floor, RC examined the bastard.

Charlee staggered to her feet, taking in the destruction of the room. What was going on?

Walking through the wreckage, she froze in horror. One of the men was not dead; he lay on the ground with his gun pointed at RC's back. She had to do something fast before he pulled the trigger. Frantically she looked around for a weapon, something to throw the shooter off. She couldn't lose RC again.

Something silver under a nearby cushion caught her attention. She grabbed the gun and without hesitation, aimed it at the man about to pull the trigger.

One thing Gran had taught her growing up; never aim a loaded weapon unless you're willing to shoot.

"What the fuck!" RC ducked when the bullet left the chamber.

The attacker hit the floor with a hole in the forehead.

"Hot damn. I need to get me one of those!" A cowboy with a straw hat entered, eyeing her up and down.

She pointed the gun at him. "Don't move."

"Sure thing, sheriff." The bastard stood with his hands in the air. "I surrender."

***

"Charlee, put the gun down." RC strode to Charlee. She'd just saved his ass.

He took the pistol from her trembling hands, then wrapped his arms around her. "Are you all right?"

"He was going to shoot you, RC."

"Who, Tibbs? Nah. He's my roommate."

"No." She swatted his chest. "Are you in some kind of trouble?"

"Uh…I hate to break up this loving feeling, but we need to blow this joint before it's too late," Tibbs interrupted.

RC grabbed Charlee's hand and headed for the door, but he felt her resist. "I'm not going anywhere until you tell me what's going on."

He wished he knew, but right now he needed to get his girl out of here. He kissed her hand. "Baby, I'll tell you everything later. Right now you need to trust me. I'm not leaving here without you."

He could see the confusion in her eyes. Everything was happening so fast. Hell, she'd just seen a ghost.

"Okay."

RC led her out of the room and Tibbs followed.

With his heart beating as fast as a hunted rabbit, RC quickly took the stairs, pushing his way through the panicked mob, who were running in all directions.

"It's about fucking time, Tibbs!" Kit shouted over the noise, holding his right hand.

"Lay off, man. We had two bloodsuckers upstairs," Tibbs said.

"We need to get to the truck. Clay's pulling it around back," Kit hissed in pain.

"We're not going to make it out the front door," RC said. "They have it blocked."

"I know a way." Charlee tugged RC toward the stage. "Follow me."

The four of them dodged backstage. They followed Charlee through the dressing room, stepping over broken chairs and glass. Shit! Who was behind this attack? Whoever it was, they meant business.

"Oh dear God!" Charlee yelled.

RC looked over at Charlee as she dropped to her knees next to a redhead with three bullet holes in her chest. He kneeled down and felt for a pulse. "She's gone."

"No, Gia." Charlee covered her mouth.

"We have to keep moving, Charlee." When she didn't respond, RC pulled her up and helped her stand. "Look at me. We need to get out of here, now. Are you with me?"

Charlee looked at him with a blank stare. She was losing it.

RC motioned for Tibbs and Kit to run ahead while he removed Charlee from her friend. As soon as they stepped outside, Clay's truck came to a screeching halt right in front of them. RC opened the door and shoved Charlee into the backseat and dove in next to her. As soon as the last door slammed shut, Clay took off like a bat out of hell.

For a moment everything was quiet. RC ran his fingers through Charlee's hair while she rested her head on his shoulder. He leaned his head back and listened to her beating heart, relieved nothing had happened to her. For now, he'd pretend all was right in the universe. He had his girl in his arms and nothing stood between them. Fuck reality! It could wait.

Clay broke the silence. "How many were there?"

Tibbs stared out the window. "I blasted two fuckers on my way upstairs to RC."

"I took out three," Clay said. "How about you, Kit?"

"I got one and another one fled."

"And you, RC?" Clay asked.

"Two." RC kissed Charlee's head.

"Hold up," Tibbs said as he turned around in the front seat. "The Lone Ranger over here saved your ass." He grinned at Charlee.

"What?" Clay glanced at them through the rearview mirror. "No. Hell no!" Clay brought the truck to a screeching halt on the side of the road.

Bracing himself against the force of the stop, RC gripped the back of the passenger seat. "What the hell, Clay?"

"The blonde has to go," Clay demanded.

"What do you mean?" RC glared at the back of Clay's head.

"No humans are allowed underground. Roman will shit."

"If Charlee goes, so do I. She's with me." He reached for the truck door.

"Hoss, stop being an asshole. We can't leave her here without knowing why the club was targeted. She could be in danger." Kit turned to Charlee and offered her his hand. "By the way, I'm Kit."

She shook his hand. "Charlee."

"The mule up front with his shorts in a wad is Clay and the one ogling your…" he nodded to her breasts, "that's Tibbs."

"Howdy." Tibbs tipped his hat and smiled like a kid in a candy shop.

"For God's sake!" RC's fingers flew down his shirt, unbuttoning the damn thing. "Show some respect." He draped the button-down around Charlee's shoulders, shielding her body from view.

"Fine." Clay shoved the truck into gear. "You're dealing with Roman on this one, *not me*." He pealed out as he merged with the traffic again.

Right now, RC couldn't give a rat's ass about Roman's rules. He pulled Charlee close, feeling her warmth pressed against his skin. Yeah, they had a lot of time to make up for. He whispered in her ear, "Get some sleep, baby. I'll take care of everything." Once he felt her body relax, his brain went into overdrive, trying to think of a way to tell her about his change. She'd have questions, and he didn't know how many he could answer.

Chapter Six

Hours ticked away. Exactly how many, RC didn't know. He was back at the Hell's Cowboys compound with Charlee sleeping next to him in his bed. She hadn't moved since she'd fallen asleep in the truck. He'd carried her straight to his room and tucked her in bed, where she'd slept like she hadn't rested in days.

With nowhere else he wanted to be, he slipped in next to her, watching her. She was lying on her side facing him, with her long dark eyelashes resting on her cheeks. Her lips were a temptation hard to resist. He'd do anything to taste her again. He traced a finger down her cheek and lifted a lock of her hair. Scooting closer, he breathed in her scent.

The soft fragrance reminded him of the huge magnolia tree in his front yard as a kid. They spent many summers underneath that tree, dreaming and sharing peanut butter and jelly sandwiches. That's where he kissed her for the first time. Man, he'd never forget the hot summer breeze blowing through her hair, carrying that sweet scent.

He rolled over on his back, folding his hands under his head, fighting the urge to wake her up and make love. It had been so long and he'd missed her like crazy—every day since he'd disappeared. Reliving their old life, tasting her again, burying himself balls deep inside her … fuck. He needed Charlee in every way, but it could never be.

Fate had altered their dreams. He wasn't the same boy, the one who picked flowers for her and took her to their high school prom. Those memories were lost. He'd been reborn as a creature who she could never love or understand. He was the man who would break her heart all over again.

A memory of the night he'd let Charlee go settled over him. She'd been surprised; never saw it coming when he told her to move on, to go to college and make something of herself. She deserved a better life than what he could provide at the time. The hurt in her eyes branded his mind forever.

Her soft hand touched his chest. He turned his head, staring into the most stunning blue eyes he'd ever seen.

"Hey," Charlee said listlessly.

RC smiled. "Hey."

As beautiful as an angel; he couldn't look away. And the more her gaze roamed freely over his body… "What? Stop looking at me like that."

Charlee tucked her hands under her pillow. "I can't believe you're alive. I thought I'd wake and you'd be a dream."

He caressed her cheek. "I've ached for you every day, Charlee girl." He swiped a tear from her cheek.

"Kiss me," she whispered.

He held her cheek and slowly leaned in, brushing his lips against hers. She opened for him and he sought out the kiss he'd dreamed about for years. Their tongues glided together, devouring the passion that waited to be released. Even though they'd only scratched the surface of their reunion, RC knew it couldn't go any further. He had to tell her everything before they could move on.

It took all his will to break the kiss, though he couldn't resist touching her. He rested his forehead against hers. Her leg brushed his cock and he groaned.

"I missed this." Her hand trailed down his chest and he grabbed it before she crossed the state line.

"Charlee." He exhaled. "We... can't do this. Why don't we just rest?"

He felt her glare straight to his soul. Charlee sat up, curling her legs underneath her. "I don't want to sleep, RC. I want to know what kind of trouble you're in. Who were those men at the club trying to kill you? Have you been in hiding because of them?"

He stared at the ceiling and cursed himself for what he was about to do, but it had to be done. A diversion was needed until he figured out how to explain the situation. He crawled out of bed, unable to think straight, being this close to her. Losing his resolve, he shoved his hands through his hair and paced at the foot of the bed. "Charlee, why the hell are you strippin' at that club? Does Gran know?"

Taken aback by his sudden change in tone, Charlee leapt from the bed and grabbed RC's arm so he'd stop pacing and look at her. "Who the hell are you to pass judgment, Mr. I-need-you-out-of-my-life-so-I-can-chase-down-my-next-bull-ride? If I recall correctly, you left me, RC."

"It wasn't like that."

"The hell it wasn't. For the past two years it's been nothing but heartache. Gran got sick and I had to quit college and come home to help her, then you…died." She took a deep breath. "I'm doing everything I can to keep the one thing I have left, and that's Gran's ranch. So, to answer your question, no, Gran doesn't know what I'm doing. She passed away right after…" Charlee broke down before she could finish the sentence.

Fuck. The damn waterworks got him every time. He tried to wrap his arms around her, but she jerked away.

"No." Charlee stomped to the door. "I don't care what kind of trouble you're in. Leave me out of it."

"Charlee, wait. Don't I get a chance to explain?" RC sprinted to the door, but it was too late, she'd already opened the door to the living room he shared with Tibbs. He grabbed her arm, meeting her stare as she turned around. "I forbid you to leave," he growled next to her ear.

She eyed his hand on her arm, and his heart froze. By the look on her face, she wasn't up for negotiations.

Clay stepped into the room. He tipped his hat to Charlee, then glared at RC. "Roman wants to talk to us. Now."

"Give me two seconds, Clay." He turned back to Charlee. "This isn't over."

She folded her arms across her chest. "I want to go home."

"Kit," Clay called.

"Hoss," Kit answered from the living room.

"Can you escort this young lady to her house?"

"I reckon I can." Kit got off the sofa and grabbed the car keys on the counter.

"Clay, I can take care of Charlee when we get back. I don't think—"

"That's right rookie, it's not your job to think." Clay took Charlee's hand and guided her out of the room.

RC followed them. "Charlee!"

She looked over her shoulder and glared at him.

"Be careful. I'll see you soon." He watched her walk out the door with Kit.

Frustrated, he pounded his fist on the doorframe.

"Well, that didn't go as planned, did it?" Tibbs said, standing at the kitchen, sipping from a cup of coffee.

"Shut up, Tibbs." RC stormed back into his bedroom, fetching a shirt and his hat. No one kept Roman waiting.

Chapter Seven

"I want to know what happened out there tonight," Roman demanded. "Val and Vin told me what went down at the club."

RC, Clay and Tibbs stood in front of his desk.

"We were minding our own business until we heard gunfire upstairs," Clay explained. "Kit, Tibbs, and myself were attacked by at least six bloodsuckers."

"And where were you?" Roman asked RC.

"In V.I.P. when I was attacked by two suckers."

Roman raised a brow. "What were you doing upstairs?"

"It's not like that," RC said, keeping his gaze ahead.

"Then would you enlighten me about the stripper? You know the rules."

RC's blood boiled, hearing his girl called a stripper. He looked at Roman. "She's an old friend. I couldn't leave her in danger, so I brought her back here. I know I shouldn't—"

Roman smacked the desk. "I don't want to hear any more excuses. You fucked up."

No shit. But for Charlee, he'd break every last rule to ensure her safety.

"You're in luck, son." Roman reclined his chair. "Val and Vin reassured me that she's not a threat."

Of course she wasn't. Nothing was going to happen to her.

"Val tells me they have never seen these men at the club before." Roman steepled his fingers under his chin. "Do we know anything about them?"

"Kit told me one got away," Clay said. "I'm sure he'll have some intel soon."

"Where's Kit?" Roman asked.

"He's—"

"I'm right here." Kit walked into the office and removed his hat.

"The rest of you leave us. We're done here." Roman stood and walked to the front of his desk. "Oh, by the way, I don't want y'all back at the club until we clean this mess up. You're on lockdown. No one leaves the compound until we know more about these thugs."

RC glared at Roman but knew better than to argue. *Lockdown?* And how was he going to stay away from Charlee? How long could he withstand not seeing her again? He gave himself a day, tops, before he'd crack.

RC followed Clay and Tibbs, but stopped next to Kit. "Is she home safely?"

Kit nodded. "All safe and tucked in."

RC squeezed the Cowboy's shoulder. "Thank you."

***

Kit took a seat, resting his elbows on his knees. How long was Roman going to make him wait for his ass chewing? He had failed him in letting the enemy escape. Truth be told, the fucker hadn't bested him; he'd let him go on purpose. He wanted the bloodsucker crawling back to his brood, warning them who was coming after them. He was tired of hiding behind Roman's conservative way of operating. Time to shit or get off the pot. And he was ready to do some ass kicking.

"I want to know everything about these assholes." Roman handed him a stack of photographs. "These are images from the security footage from the club. I want to know who they work for, when their last meal was, when they took their last shit. I want full details. Understand?"

"Loud and clear, Hoss."

Kit thumbed through the images, holding back the rising snarl of disgust he felt from picture to picture.

"Clay tells me one of the men got away," Roman said, crossing his arms over his chest.

Kit nodded. "I was taken off guard."

"It's not like you to miss a shot."

Kit peered up from the stack of photos. "Look Roman, everyone is entitled to a bad day."

"Not a Hell's Cowboy."

Falling silent, Kit stared at the floor.

"Did you set up surveillance at the stripper's house? I want us to keep a close eye on her until we figure out who these men are."

"Yes sir, inside and out."

"Good," Roman said. "Listen, I don't know now what's going on inside that head of yours, but you'd best tread softly, son. Everyone has their demons to fight, but I'm not one of them."

Adjusting his Stetson, Kit gathered the images and stood. "Are we done here? I have work to do."

"*I'm* done."

Thank Christ, because Kit couldn't stand being idle even for a short amount of time. He needed to be behind his command station checking surveillance footage, and uncovering downtown Diablo's mysteries.

Kit was almost home free when Roman started up again. "By the way, you should have Selene check your injury."

Shit. Kit looked down at his wounded shoulder. Blood had seeped through the bandage and onto his shirt. "I'd rather eat dirt," Kit said as he walked out of the office and into the elevator.

As the doors closed, he pivoted on his heels, slamming the back of his head against the wall. Roman was suspicious; he saw it in his eyes. Boss knew he'd let the bloodsucker go on purpose. Lucky for him, he'd be spending the next few days buried in the cyber world, trying to get a lead on the attackers, and off Roman's radar. All he needed was a date with a strong pot of coffee and a carton of cigarettes, and he could go for days nonstop.

The silver doors glided open with a hiss. Kit faced the door, ready to exit, but his whole body tensed. Waves of ebony hair framed a face he knew all too well. A tight white tank top and ass-hugging jeans suggested she was out for blood. There was a time he would have enjoyed being her latest victim, but not anymore. Her lips spread into a wicked red smile, rendering him speechless. Damn if the Devil wasn't a woman in red cowgirl boots.

"Hi, darlin'," Selene greeted him.

Gathering what was left of his composure before he did something stupid, like pin her inside the elevator and fuck her senseless, Kit casually tipped his hat, shouldering past her.

"You're hurt."

"Not your problem," Kit said.

"Stop being a horse's ass and let me help you. I can tell you've lost a lot of blood."

In a flash, Kit had Selene restrained against the wall. Holding her hands above her head, he pressed his body alongside hers and inhaled her exotic, tropical scent. He nuzzled her neck. Mouth watering, his fangs throbbed and extended, begging to sink deep into her hot flesh, tasting her once again. Driving his point home, he pushed his hard cock into her stomach. "You've done enough."

With a seductive thrust, she moved her body against his. "I can take care of that for you, too." She licked the tip of his nose, adding more fire to his already kindling desire.

Kit held her icy stare, knowing damn well she got off on playing with his emotions, watching him squirm beneath her relentless spell. He'd called her bluff many times and quite frankly, the game was beginning to bore him.

"One day, I hope you find your heart, and when you do, I'll drive a stake right through it." Kit pushed away from her and headed for his lab, leaving her behind—and thank the gods—speechless for once.

Chapter Eight

Mace Wrathmore stood in front of the tri-fold mirror, securing his diamond encrusted cufflinks and admiring his close shave. The white dress-shirt he wore was ironed just the way he liked it—crisp collar and crease free. Crawley, the butler, assisted Mace into his Italian-made suit jacket, smoothing out the fabric across his broad shoulders. "Sir, may I say you look like a million bucks?"

Mace shrugged into the dark blue sleeves. Damn, he wore the tailored pashmina like a true Business Vamp. "Just a million?" He turned from side to side, admiring his perfection. "Call Dario and tell him I'm not satisfied with his new collection. I need to look like a billion bucks." He flashed his fangs at the butler.

Crawley scurried out of the walk-in closet to obey his master's orders.

A snicker coming from outside the dressing room caught Mace's attention. "You're so mean to Crawley."

Walking out of the closet, Mace met Asa, his go-to vamp, sitting on a couch with his legs casually crossed, flipping through a Diablo Life magazine. The male's arrogance was irritating him this morning. Asa had fucked up and now he had the nerve to act like it meant nothing.

He pulled a cigarette from a case, then lit it. "I pay the man six figures. I expect competency. Is this too much to ask?"

"I guess it could be worse; he hasn't been eaten…yet." Asa smirked.

Mace took a long draw from his cigarette. "Please." He exhaled, filling the room with smoke. "I prefer spicier blood." He tossed the gold and chrome lighter on the table.

Needing something stronger to maintain his composure, he moved to the bar filled with soothing remedies. He'd kept Asa waiting for at least two hours as he primped himself. It was his way of getting his point across that he wasn't pleased with the current situation. Six of his men were dead and one had barely made it through Asa's interrogation. When a plan was put into action, he expected good results.

Wrathmore Enterprise controlled Diablo, Texas. His company invested in land development, commercial and residential real estate groups, the Diablo Sanitation Department for the times when he needed to take out the trash, and he always had a handful of lawyers in his back pocket. The more humans he corrupted, the more powerful he became.

Living in such a metropolis, resources were abundant. The more sin and debauchery he created, the more vampires thrived. The utmost powerful, well-respected and feared persona above-ground and the dark prince of the underworld, there was no resistance when it came to his demands. His lips curled up into a wicked grin, thinking about the influence he held.

But there was an ongoing battle with Roman and his coven. Their mission to save the half-breeds was laughable at best. No, it wasn't a mission. It was a mistake and an act of treason against vampires. Their mess needed to be cleaned up, and now he was left to destroy Diablo's half-breeds.

He poured two servings of Scotch, then made his way back to the couch. If he wanted something done right, he had to do it himself. That's why Plan B had been set into motion two days ago. Mace handed Asa a tumbler and sat down next to him, crossing his legs.

"I'm troubled, Asa." He sipped the amber liquor. "I sent out seven males under your supervision to take care of business and it doesn't please me that six of my best are now dead."

Asa leaned forward. "The operation wasn't as simple as we thought."

"She's a human. It doesn't get much easier than that!" Mace slammed his glass on the table, causing Asa to flinch. He closed his eyes and inhaled. Mace channeled his inner peace and composed himself. *Control.*

"We didn't expect to be ambushed by a group of Hell's Cowboys."

Slowly, Mace opened his eyes at the mention of the half-breeds.

"The girl was with one of the Cowboys."

"How many were there?" Mace asked.

"Four."

The tension in the room was thick. Mace got off on making his men squirm, anticipating his reactions. He took a long drag of his cigarette. "You'll need to replace those soldiers. Do you understand?"

"Yes, sir."

Mace called out to a black cylinder speaker sitting in the corner. "Hilary, call Charlee Brysen."

The robotic cyber voice responded. "Yes, Master Wrathmore, calling Charlee Brysen."

"Thank you, Hilary."

"My pleasure, sir."

"See, Asa, compliance."

"Hello?" Her voice was as sweet as candy.

"Miss Brysen, Mace Wrathmore."

"Oh. Hi."

"I haven't caught you at a bad time, have I?"

"No, I'm good. How can I help you, Mr. Wrathmore?"

He almost felt insulted that a woman would forget about a date with him, but she was human. He'd let it slide. "Please, call me Mace. Are we still on for tonight?"

"Tonight?"

"Oh, don't tell me you've forgotten."

"No, no, I haven't forgotten. It's just a lot has happened in the past two days and—"

"Good, I'll pick you up at eight o'clock."

"Mace, I—"

"Until then, Miss Brysen."

Mace ended the phone call and smiled in victory. Yes, he'd have to sacrifice his night to play instead of dealing with the stack of papers on his desk back at the office, which irked him. But in this case he was eager for his meeting with Miss Brysen and was confident he'd get the job done. It never hurt mixing business with pleasure when a beautiful woman was involved.

Normally he conducted business at night, downtown in his high-rise office, and preferred spending the day underground. It was safer that way, but not always productive, since most of his interactions were with humans. The way underground Diablo was constructed, most tunnels led to covered parking garages, making it easier for a vampire to travel during the day. In every office building and limo that Mace owned he had a special barrier installed on all windows that blocked out ultraviolet rays, allowing him to walk freely and function like a human. Only able to withstand the sunlight for so long, if he didn't take care, his skin would blister and burn. Mace couldn't run his business efficiently if he was hot under the collar.

Mace slipped on his polarized Aviator sunglasses, before he made his way into the dreaded sunlight. He needed to get to the office and attend to business before his date with the human. He stood and adjusted his suit jacket. "Asa, let this be a lesson learned. I always get what I want."

"Yes, Sir." Asa stood and left the room.

Chapter Nine

Charlee stared at her cellphone, wondering what had just happened. She'd forgotten about her encounter with Mace Wrathmore a couple days ago at the finance department of Diablo Central Bank. One last plea and one last hope, Charlee had met with her loan officer to go over her options. She was praying for a loan modification, but she was too far behind in payments, there was nothing the officer could do to help her.

Defeated, she'd gathered her paperwork, stuffing it into a folder and left the cubicle. She han't been paying attention as she walked across the main lobby to leave, and bumped right into Mace Wrathmore, spilling late notices and foreclosure warnings all over the floor. To make the situation worse, she collided with his forehead as they both bent down to retrieve the papers. After an awkward introduction, he must have felt sorry for her and offered to buy her a coffee at the upstairs cafeteria.

She still didn't know what had come over her, opening up like a punctured vein and bleeding out her troubles the way she had. It was strange how comfortable she'd felt discussing her problems with a stranger, which wasn't like her at all. But he genuinely seemed to care and listened to her, unlike her loan officer. So when Mace asked her out for a friendly dinner to discuss her options, the fight in her couldn't resist the temptation to at least hear him out.

Charlee sat down at the kitchen table and wrapped her hands around a hot cup of tea. What was she going to do? She walked a fine line of desperation. More so now that the club was shut down and under investigation for the rest of the week. Seven days was a lot of potential money lost and meant another late payment.

She exhaled and leaned back into the chair. Yeah, two days had passed and no word from RC. Should it surprise her?

She'd really come down hard on him. She hadn't realized how much she blamed him for her troubles, until he lashed out. He'd broken her heart and crushed her dreams the day he'd left her for the damn rodeo. All she wanted to do was love him. He'd pulled back his bow and released the fatal arrow straight to her heart, destroying her. At first the heartache made it unbearable to even get out of bed. Gran had told her once she moved into the dorm and settled into her course load, she'd forget that RC Reid even existed. She'd tried, but life wasn't the same without him. And then he died.

He'd faked his own death? The tears she'd shed over him had been wasted. He'd lied. Abandoned her and anyone else who cared. The guilt she carried for staying away from home had been wasted time she could never get back. Precious time away from Gran. A lump formed in her throat. All along he was alive and well. Denying that she was happy to see him alive would be a lie. As soon as their bodies touched, she'd remembered why it hurt so much to lose him before.

Obviously the attackers from the club wanted him dead. But why? Did he fake his own death to escape those men and now they'd finally caught up to him? People just don't rise from the dead—he wanted to be forgotten.

She recalled leaving RC's place. Kit had blindfolded her before they left the parking garage and warned her, "If you value your life, you won't peek." Who lives in a place so secretive?

Thinking about how scared she'd been sitting blindfolded in the passenger side of Kit's truck, still made her heart race.

She had to find out what kind of trouble RC was mixed up in. She deserved an answer—closure.

Charlee glanced at the clock on the microwave and flew out of the chair. She hadn't been on a date in a long time. She needed to check her closet for a dress to wear and hopefully she'd have shoes to match.

She started up the stairs, then stopped when someone knocked. Hank, her blue Australian cattle dog, jolted from his bed next to the fireplace and ran to the door barking.

"Hank," Charlee called out as she approached the door. She peeked out the curtain and smiled. *Jackie.* Excitedly, she unlocked the deadbolt and opened the door. She charged with open arms and hugged her tight. "Girl, you don't know how happy I am to see you."

After seeing Gia dead, Charlee had been worried about Jackie. She hadn't heard from or seen her since the shooting.

Jackie hugged her back. "Me too. I was scared to come over or call. I'd go country real on anyone who tried to hurt you."

"Come in." Charlee closed the door behind them. "You want some tea or something to eat?"

"I'd love a hot cup of tea." She placed her bag on the couch and looked around.

"Have you heard anything about the investigation?" Charlee asked from the kitchen as she placed the kettle on the stove.

"An officer stopped by the other day. I told him everything I knew, though I'm not much help. I didn't see the men enter the club, and by the time the shots rang out, the place was in chaos. Have you?"

Charlee paused as she reached into the cabinet for a mug. That night flashed before her. She was standing aiming her smoking gun at the attacker's face, watching blood pour out of a bullet hole in his forehead.

"Charlee?" Jackie called.

"What?" She set the mug on the table.

"Did you talk to the police yet?" Jackie stood in the doorway now.

"Oh, right." She shook free of the bitter memory. "No one's been by to take my statement." Charlee sat down across from Jackie.

"You know what I heard?"

"What?" Charlee's brows creased.

"I heard that six of the seven shooters were shot dead and no one can find their bodies. It's like they never existed."

"Who told you that?" Charlee didn't believe it.

"A friend," Jackie said nonchalantly.

"A friend? And what did the officer say about the shooters when they took your statement?"

"They wouldn't say anything, just asked questions."

A shrill whistle caused them both to jump. Charlee got up and took the teapot off the stove. "I don't believe it. Bodies don't just disappear."

"I know it sounds crazy."

"Well, the investigation is still ongoing. I'm sure the detectives are still piecing the evidence together." Charlee placed the steaming mug down in front of Jackie.

"I guess you're right. It's probably one of Val's deals gone bad." Jackie blew through the steam and sipped the tea. "Anyway, how are you?"

"I'm good."

Jackie raised a black brow, calling bullshit.

"Fine." She rolled her eyes. "I have a date tonight."

"Eek!" Jackie clapped her hands. "Oh girl, I have to do your hair. And makeup."

"And what's wrong with my makeup?"

"You know I love you, right? But you could use a little—you know—help with lining your eyes. A nice winged cat-eye would bring out the blue in your eyes."

"Um, thanks…I guess."

Jackie cocked her head to the side and smiled. "This will be fun. So, when is he picking you up?"

"Eight."

"Well, we better get to work." Jackie winked.

Hours later, after many failed attempts, Charlee finally agreed to Jackie's feline eye creation so long as she got to wear her hair down. Taking the hand-held mirror from her friend, she turned and checked the blonde waves of hair cascading down her back in the bathroom mirror behind her. "Wow, Jackie, it's gorgeous."

Jackie looked at the black eye-liner pencil in her hand and blew on the end. "Yes, I know. Celebrities are pounding down my door for my sexy, seductive cat-eyes."

They shared a laugh.

Charlee went to her room where the outfit Jackie had chosen was laid out on the bed. She cringed at the shoes and tight-fitting dress. She wanted to look hot, but not like she was going to work. If she wanted Mace to take her seriously, she had to dress properly.

"Okay, Char, this is when I leave you." Jackie hugged her. "I'll see my way out."

"Thanks for everything, Jackie. Seriously, I don't know what I'd do without you."

Jackie smiled and rubbed Charlee's shoulder. "Be careful out there."

"I know." Playfully she pushed Jackie out of her room.

As Jackie reached the top of the stairs she called out, "Don't do anything I wouldn't do."

Charlee rolled her eyes.

"Call me," Jackie called out again.

When she heard the front door shut, Charlee turned her attention back to the strapless, too short dress. And forget about the shoes…no way.

Remembering a cute floral sundress she'd seen Jackie pass over, Charlee went to her closet and took it off the hanger. She dropped her robe and slipped the silk fabric over her head, tugging it into place. The front of the dress was cut shorter than the back and showed off her long, slender legs. Even though this was strictly a business date, she'd use her assets to grab Mace's attention, and hopefully save her Gran's ranch. At least she'd be comfortable in her clothes tonight. The thought of constantly pulling and fidgeting with that black spandex made her want to put on her nightgown and crawl back to bed.

With a last makeup check, she grabbed her pink cowboy boots and jean jacket, then headed downstairs. If her sneaking suspicion was right, Mace would promptly arrive at eight and she didn't want to keep him waiting.

Hank lifted his head a few minutes later, alerting Charlee of her date's arrival. A loud knock sounded.

She was right…eight o'clock.

She opened the door and suddenly couldn't form a word. Her mouth went dry and her body went numb as she took in Mace Wrathmore standing in his tailored suit on her front porch. Bona fide, sexy billionaire sophistication at its best. Chiseled, clean-shaven jawline, suave expression, and charcoal eyes. Mace sure knew how to make a woman squirm in her panties. Even his disheveled hair appeared to be perfection.

"Are you going to invite me in?" God, even his tone was somewhere between velvet and chocolate—deep and smooth.

"Of course, come in." Embarrassed for staring too long, Charlee shook her head as she stepped back to let him pass.

Hank stood at attention next to Charlee, growling.

"Um, your dog isn't going to attack me, is he?"

What? Oh, for the love of... "Hank," she scolded. "Go lay down. Mr. Wrathmore is our guest."

"Mace, please."

"Yes, I'm so sorry. I'll grab my jacket and we can go."

"Not so fast," Mace smiled, teeth gleaming. "These are for you." He offered her a bouquet of red roses.

Charlee stepped forward and took the roses, smelling the buds. "These are gorgeous, Mace, thank you. I'll go put them in some water." Feeling awkward, she turned on her heels and went into the kitchen. As she moved away from Mace she felt the fog of lust lifting and she could think straight. What was going on? She'd dealt with many businessmen at the club, she knew how to handle them; yet Mace had a different effect on her.

He exhibited power to the fullest; his stance was dominating, dripping with sex appeal, the typical appearance one would expect to encounter from a high-profile man. However, danger lurked behind those dark eyes; something haunting, soul-shaking. Red alert warnings were going off left and right. She just hoped the first responders could resuscitate her, because a man like Mace Wrathmore could chew her up and spit her out without blinking an eye.

Charlee, he's just a man. You can handle him.

On the kitchen table, Charlee set down a vase and quickly arranged the roses. Before returning to her guest, she ran her fingers through her hair and fidgeted with the straps on her dress. She inhaled, trying to calm herself as she made her way back to Mace.

He had her jacket, offering to help her into it. She smiled and accepted his offer.

"Shall we?" Mace motioned toward the door.

Like a true gentleman, he opened the passenger door to his steel-blue Aston Martin, inviting her into his domain equipped with black leather trappings, and smelling every bit of two hundred grand.

As Mace sank down into the driver's seat, his shoulder brushed again hers making her completely aware of how close they were. From the corner of her eye she noticed him looking at her thighs. Her body heated under his smolder. *This man is dangerous.*

"May I say, you look rather divine tonight." He took another glance at her legs.

Seductively, she crossed them, and covered her thigh. Calm and confident, she tipped his chin, bringing his eyes back on hers. "Mace, it's not nice to stare. If you can't treat me like a lady, this date is over."

"You're right. From here on out I promise to be good." He started the ignition and drove down the winding gravel road.

The conversation during dinner was interesting, if you wanted to know which buildings he owned in downtown Diablo. She got the point he was a wealthy man after the fifth law firm had been mentioned. Charlee picked at a carrot in her salad as her thoughts drifted elsewhere—RC Reid. She wondered where he was tonight and if he was staying out of trouble. She wished it was her cowboy sitting across from her, telling her how much he missed her; making plans for the future.

The ambiance was stunning; she'd never dined on top of a high rise before. Twinkling lights lined the roof's edge, and glowed softly against the night sky. A gentle breeze blew through the private alcove where they sat, flickering the candle flames as they ate their dinner salads, finally uninterrupted by the wait staff. Charlee found it rather excessive for five people to be waiting on them.

Mace sipped his Merlot, eyeing Charlee from over the brim of the wine glass. "You don't like carrots?"

She laid down her fork. "I'm sorry. I have a lot on my mind."

"Is there something you want to talk about?" He set the wine glass down and gave her his full attention.

Charlee didn't know where to start or how much to tell. She kept her troubles to herself, but there he was again being sincere. "I don't want to burden you with my problems. Things always have a way of working out." She picked up her fork and began eating, then she noticed he hadn't touched his salad. "Aren't you hungry?"

Mace smirked, apparently amused by her comment. "Charlee, I have an offer for you that I think will help you in your situation." He reached inside his suit pocket and pulled out a folded set of papers. "I want to buy your ranch." He flattened the papers on the table. "I'm willing to pay triple what it's worth."

Triple! Charlee coughed, choking on a crouton. She grabbed a glass of water and drank.

"Are you alright?" Mace began to stand.

She waved her hand for him to sit down. "I'm fine." She cleared her throat. "That's very generous of you, but I can't accept."

"And why not?" Mace sounded perturbed that his offer had been so quickly refused.

"My gran left the ranch to me when she passed away. It's where I grew up and all I have left. It's my home." Charlee looked down into her lap. It was all she had left worth fighting for.

Mace reached across the table and took her hand in his. "I didn't mean to upset you. I'm trying to help. Look, I'm not going to act like I knew your Gran, but would she want you to suffer just to keep the ranch?" He circled her wrist with his thumb. "What would she think if she knew you were stripping to keep out of foreclosure?"

Charlee arched a brow and her heart sunk. How did he know she was a stripper? She hadn't shared that intimate piece of information with him. Slowly she glided her hand away from his grip.

"There comes a time when you have to do what's right for you. With the money I'm offering you'll be well set for the rest of your life."

"Wait, how do you know I'm a stripper?" Charlee reluctantly asked.

He leaned back and crossed his legs. "I know everything that happens in Diablo. I am the heart and soul of Diablo, Texas, sweetheart."

Chapter Ten

RC was going out of his damn mind. The rhythmic sound of the tennis ball bouncing off the wall did nothing to soothe his nerves. Thud after thud, he whipped that yellow fucker harder with each throw. Nothing. Stuck in lockdown at the Cowboys' compound, all he could think about was Charlee: her dancing, in his bed, her icy glare before she left with Kit. *Fuck*! Showing no mercy, he flung the ball faster.

He'd begged Clay for the keys to his truck. When Clay didn't budge, he'd turned the place upside down looking for them but it was useless; they were on lockdown and he wasn't getting out of there anytime soon. When begging didn't work, he'd checked in with Kit, and hovered over his shoulder, watching the surveillance monitors dedicated to Charlee's house. Kit eventually kicked his ass out for excessive badgering, complaining that he couldn't do his job with him breathing down his neck. Two days had passed, and there were no leads on the gunmen. RC's jaw clenched thinking about the fuckers.

"If you don't stop throwing that fucking ball, I'm going to hog tie your ass." Tibbs shuffled out of his bedroom and into the kitchen, wearing nothing but boxer briefs.

RC ignored the Cowboy.

"Damn it." Tibbs stepped between RC and the wall, catching the ball.

"What the hell?" RC shot up.

"Uptight much?" Tibbs squeezed the ball so hard it popped, then threw it on the floor.

RC ran his hands through his hair. "I'm going insane. I should be with Charlee. She's in danger, I feel it."

"Nah, Kit has her wired up good." Tibbs headed back into the kitchen, scratching his ass. "Cereal?"

"I'm good."

For a moment he admired Tibbs. The Cowboy worried about nothing. For once he wished he could be as free, but he wasn't, and he didn't trust that security system to keep his Charlee girl safe. The only thing that could ensure her wellbeing was himself.

Tibbs sat down next to him. "I wish I had a good girl to come home to." He handed RC his truck keys. "Go get your girl."

RC glanced at Tibbs, surprised. "But—"

Tibbs waved him on as he munched on a mouthful of corn flakes. "If anyone asks, I haven't seen you all morning."

RC took the keys and stood.

Tibbs rested his feet on the table, flipping through the cable channels. "Oh, you have about ten minutes before Clay gets back from the gym. I can only stall him for so long."

With that said, RC grabbed his cowboy hat and rope, and left the compound, praying he'd stay clear of Clay.

***

She's not home. RC pulled the keys out of the ignition. It was after ten PM and Charlee's vehicle wasn't in the driveway. "Where could she be?"

He got out and headed to the white, two-story farmhouse. Time had weathered the exterior paint, but the soft pink front door was still inviting like he remembered. How many kisses had he stolen from Charlee at the door? He missed those days so much.

RC took his time making his way to the front porch, taking in all the memories he'd left behind. Two wooden rocking chairs sat to the left of the door, creaking with the light breeze. He remembered Gran sitting on one of the rocking chairs, waiting for him to bring Charlee home after their dates. And if they were late, Gran would give RC a piece of her mind, but a hug always followed. If it hadn't been for the old woman's love, he would have been a real hellion.

RC peeked inside the closest window. It was dark.

"So, when did RC Reid become a peeping tom?"

He froze. *Shit.* Charlee was standing on the bottom step of the porch with her hands on her hips, staring him down with those bright blue eyes.

"If you want to come inside, all you have to do is ask." Charlee walked up the steps to the front door and unlocked it. When RC didn't make a move, she looked at him. "You comin'?"

"Um. Yes, ma'am."

As soon as RC walked inside, Hank's ears perked up and the dog ran to him.

"Hank!" RC bent down and was greeted by wet kisses. Hank jumped in his lap, almost causing RC to fall over. "I can't believe you're still alive, ol' boy." He scratched his belly.

"When your momma sold her place, Hank wouldn't leave. So I took him in," Charlee said from the kitchen.

"Figures. She'd sell her soul if the price was right. We didn't have much, but damn she could have at least kept our home." He stood, adjusting his hat.

Charlee walked into the living room and handed him a beer. "She didn't have anyone to pass the property to, RC. She thought you were dead."

Everyone believed he was buried six feet under. "Thanks for saving Hank."

"He's a good boy." Charlee smiled at the dog who was happier than a pig in shit, wagging his tail.

Not much had changed in Charlee's house. The floral couch where Charlee and he'd made out as teenagers still sat in the same place. He imagined the fire crackling and seeing her naked silhouette. It all came rushing back to him as if it were yesterday. Damn, what he wouldn't do to go back in time, to be inside her again.

But things had changed between them. Charlee was so different, but familiar at the same time. If that made any damn sense.

"Charlee, we need to talk, sweetheart."

"I'm all ears." She wrapped her lips around the beer bottle and took a long pull.

Damn, this woman was already digging his grave. He watched her neck as she swallowed and imagined himself placing kisses below her ear. Her hair was curled in long strands cascading over her bare shoulders. His eyes traveled down her floral sundress. He itched to rip the silk off her body and have those long, tanned legs wrapped around his waist. How was he supposed to think clearly when his cock was doing the thinking for him? Wait, why was she in a dress and out late?

His brows creased. "Where were you tonight?"

Charlee rolled her eyes. "If you must know I was out on a date."

"A date?"

"Look, I'm tired. Get to the point. Why are you here?"

It was time to fess up and tell her everything about the break up and his fatal last bull ride. She wasn't the only one who had changed. Breaking her heart all over again could very well be the death of him.

He had to tread softly here; one wrong word and she'd throw his ass out faster than fuck. "Charlee, I've changed."

"If this is another lame ass excuse to make you feel better for leaving and lying to me again, I've already been there, so don't let the door hit you where the good Lord split ya on the way out."

RC grabbed her arm before she could walk away. He pulled her close and growled in her ear, "It's not like that. Please, give me a chance to explain. If you want to throw me out after, then do it. I'll never bother you again."

She slipped out of his grip and crossed her arms. "Fine. My bullshit radar is charged and ready."

"Fair enough," he agreed. "Sit." He gestured at the sofa.

"I'd rather not." She crossed her arms over her chest.

"Fine." RC sat down, resting his elbows on his thighs. "It's true, something has changed me. I'm no longer the person you once knew. That night at the rodeo, I died. The bull rider you knew, the one who was fighting his way through his rookie year to make it to the championship to win the million-dollar prize money is long gone. He died right there in that arena trying to make something of himself so his girl would be proud to call him her husband. He did everything for you. What he didn't know, was that he'd run out of time before he could tell you he was a damn fool for letting you go." RC glanced at Charlee. "I only wanted the best for you, Charlee. I didn't want you to give up your dreams to chase mine. I mean yes, I wanted you with me, but you had a chance to go to college and become something."

"RC…"

"No." He rubbed his sweaty palms on his jeans. "Let me finish. There's a part of me that I didn't know existed until that night. The signs were there, but I didn't know to look for them." He sucked in a deep breath; there was no holding back. "This is going to sound crazy, sweetheart." He took a deep breath, holding it hostage in his lungs as he held her gaze, then forced the words from his lips. "I'm a half-breed, a dhampir. I'm part human, part vampire."

He expected Charlee to bust out laughing and call bullshit, but she just sat there, silent and emotionless. The poor girl was in shock.

"It's more complicated than even I know, but my father was a vampire and maw was human. I know! It's crazy, but that's how it works with dhampirs." RC shrugged his shoulders. "RC Reid died in that arena, Charlee. What's left, what you see in front of you, it's still me, but different. I've spent the last two years in training, like boot camp, learning how to deal with all this and how to protect our kind from extermination."

Charlee's eyes grew wide. Finally, a response.

"It's a long, complicated story. Bottom line, I never intended to hurt you, Charlee girl. The more I wanted to provide for you, the harder I failed."

RC's heart was ready to plummet out of his chest if she didn't say something soon. The anticipation was eating him alive. "I know this is a lot to take in, but I couldn't go another day without telling you. Please, baby, say something. Hit me. Hell, kick me in the balls. Throw my ass out. Do something."

Charlee took a step back. "I can't believe it. I finally have you back and you've lost your damn mind." She took another step back, keeping a watchful eye on him until she bumped into the coffee table. Taking her eyes off him for a brief second, she reached into her purse and pulled out her cell phone.

"Hey Siri," she spoke into her phone.

"I'm listening…" the device replied.

"What are you doing, Charlee?" RC questioned her odd behavior.

"Number for Diablo county mental health crisis hotline."

RC bolted from the couch and grabbed the cell out of Charlee's hands. He pulled her close; her body was trembling. "I'm not insane. I'm telling you the truth. Not even I could make this shit up." He glared down into her blue depths. "I'm still me."

"RC, I don't know what to believe anymore. One day you're dead, the next alive and now you think you're a freaking vampire."

He flashed her his fangs and all disbelief melted from her face. She lifted his lip and gasped. "Vampire?"

He'd expected her to doubt him. Words are only words. Showing her that he was the same cowboy she'd fallen in love with was the only way to reach her.

"Believe in me." He snaked his hand around to the small of her back, capturing her body against his. He dipped down and slid his tongue past her lips, commanding her to kiss him. Her lips were soft just like he remembered. Surprised she'd opened up, he deepened the kiss as she melted against him. She quivered underneath his touch and he grinned in satisfaction that his plan was working. Hell yeah, he'd missed his Charlee girl.

"Okay, I've found one location for Diablo crisis hotline. Is that the one you want?" A robotic voice came from Charlee's phone.

RC threw the damn thing on the couch while he continued to show his girl how much he'd missed her. He grabbed her ass, grinding his hardened dick into her stomach.

She placed her hand on his chest, breaking the kiss. "Hold up, cowboy," she said, out of breath. "We need to talk."

She led him to the couch where they sat side by side.

She removed his cowboy hat and set it on the coffee table. "Russel, all I ever wanted was this." Her hand moved over his heart. "I never asked for a big house or fancy things. All I ever wanted was you." RC swiped a tear from the corner of her eye. "You have always been enough for me."

He rested his forehead against hers. "Even now, knowing what I am?"

"Yes," she whispered.

He shook his head. "You should be afraid of me. I'm a monster."

"I know, but you're the boy I fell in love with. Whatever happens, I'll be right by your side. I love you."

RC took her lips in a soft kiss, but his need was quickly building into a burning hunger. "Christ, I've missed you," he breathed heavily between kisses.

He moved his hands up her thighs as she lay back on the couch. They kissed each other like they were love-struck, hormones-racing teens again. He positioned his broad body between her legs and a jolt hit his upper jaw when she wrapped her legs around him. He felt her heat and his fangs extended, elongating to a sharp point. *Fuck!* His arousal was going to cause him more harm than good. Charlee couldn't see him like this; it was too soon.

Before he did something stupid, like sink his teeth into her delicate skin, he buried his face into a pillow behind Charlee's head. God, he'd missed her touch, her hands threading through his hair, her nails raking against his scalp. His frustration only deepened when she left a fiery trail of kisses down his neck.

"What's wrong?" Charlee asked.

Once his fangs retracted, RC pushed up, resting his weight on his hands. "You want to go for a drive?"

Charlee arched a brow. "I think that's a good idea."

He helped her off the couch and adjusted his Wranglers. He needed to put some air between them. Things were heating up too quickly. Grabbing his hat, he followed Charlee out the front door.

RC drove down the winding road between what had once been his home, and Charlee's. The moon was shining bright. The night air, fresh and cool, blew in through the open windows, and he had Charlee snuggled up under his arm—nothing could be more perfect.

The truck rolled to a stop, and Charlee smiled. "How did I know you'd take me here?"

RC inhaled. The pungent magnolia fragrance brought him right back to a special place he frequently visited in his dreams. "It's *our* spot." He cut the engine, but kept the radio on. He met Charlee at the back of the truck where he spread out a blanket in the cab. He offered his hand. "My lady."

She grinned in that same heart-stopping way he remembered from when they were kids. She took his hand and he helped her into the back of the truck.

They sat and he wrapped his arm around her as she rested her head on his shoulder. If someone woke him from this dream, he'd show them no mercy. For the past two years, all he'd had were dreams to keep the hope alive that one day he'd be sitting here just like this with the woman he loved. There was a lot of lost time to make up.

"So where were you tonight?" RC fidgeted with the hem of her dress.

"The other day I bumped into this man coming out of the bank. To make a long story short, he asked me to dinner to discuss how he could help me keep my ranch."

"What do you mean, keep the ranch?"

"RC, I'm buried so deep in late mortgage payments that I don't think I'll ever see the light of day. Not to mention the back taxes I owe. Why do you think I was strippin'?"

And there it was. He knew there had to be a good reason.

"How far behind are you? I would have thought Gran was pretty well off."

"No, she had to take out a second mortgage awhile back. I'm at least a year behind."

RC leaned his head back and exhaled. "Was he able to help you?"

"Yes and no," Charlee said. "If I sell the ranch to him, he's willing to help. But I really don't want to sell, RC. This is my home."

"I know, sweetheart." He pulled her close and kissed the top of her head. "I'll figure something out so you can stay."

Charlee sat up. "RC, I can't—"

"You can and will. Let me do this for you."

Charlee shook her head and snuggled back into his chest. "Stubborn cowboy."

"Yep." Grinning like a fool, RC knew he needed to do this for her; to right the wrong.

They sat listening to the crickets chirp. Lightly, he trailed his fingers up and down Charlee's arm, content just holding her.

An electric guitar rang out over the speakers, joined by thumping bass. RC gave her a huge smile—it was Charlee's song. She'd danced to it at the club. Her body tensed and he fought back the urge to laugh.

"You know." He cleared his throat. "I never got that lap dance I paid for."

She giggled. "Well, Texas doesn't like lap dancing."

"What about Charlee?"

When she didn't respond, he thought maybe he'd taken it too far. She didn't like being a stripper. But he had to try; he wanted that private dance.

Charlee looked up at him and bit her bottom lip. "I have rules."

"Oh, you do?"

"A-ha." She sat back on her heels. "I don't get nude."

"I can handle that."

Seductively, she rose up on her knees and straddled him. She removed his Stetson. RC gazed up at her, watching her as she put on his hat. "Only I can touch the goods." She winked.

RC swallowed hard as her hands slid down his button-down, pulling it free from his jeans. He'd abide by her rules for now and let her take charge. In the end, she'd better be ready, because her ass was his.

The next thing he felt was the warm night air against his skin as Charlee tossed his shirt to the side and stood. She dipped down and swayed her hips. *Holy hell!* He balled his fists, resisting the urge to reach out, to pull her close, to bury his face between her legs. His mouth watered at the memory of her taste.

He looked up and met her gaze, gleaming down at him. With a wicked smile, she slid down his chest so he could feel every inch of her body. She knew his weakness, touching him in all the right places. Unable to resist, he gripped her ass, rubbing her sweet, hot heat along his throbbing cock. For fuck's sake, the woman drove him wild.

Charlee waggled her finger at him in playful disapproval. "Uh, uh. No touching."

"Fuck the rules," he groaned and in a flash, had Charlee on her back. The trunk bed creaked against the force of his body as he braced himself between her legs. He pressed his cock against her silk panties and passion surged through him like he'd never felt before. He was coming undone at the seams.

This would be the first time he'd tested the limits of sex as a half-breed. The human desire was still there, anticipating every move, yet something else pulsed through his veins. He wanted her to succumb to his every demand, to see her body react to his touch. Then there was an animalistic urge to taste her blood. He didn't quite understand it all, the feelings warring inside him. Perhaps he wasn't supposed to comprehend it. Maybe all he needed to do was embrace his vampire beast and just go with it, instead of resisting. He just hoped it wouldn't spiral out of his control.

He claimed a breast, sucking and nipping her skin while his hand squeezed the other. He pulled her dress up, catching a look at her slim thighs, smelling her excitement, all challenging that control. His true nature broke through, forcing his fangs to extend despite his effort to keep them hidden. He bit into her belt, tearing through the thin, decorative leather like a hot knife through butter.

"Are you scared of me now?" he said when he caught her wide-eyed gaze focused on the sharp, white fangs.

With trembling hands, Charlee caressed a fang with the tip of her finger. "Terrified."

He closed his eyes. It was too good to be true. Everything was more complicated now. He couldn't just waltz in here and pick up where they left off. He tried to retreat, but Charlie grabbed his face and pinned him with a heart-piercing glare.

"But…"

"I know you, Russel Reid, and you'd never hurt me." She rose up and softly brushed his lips with a kiss.

"I'd die before I'd ever hurt you," he whispered.

His insides were on fire when she wrapped her legs around his hips. The heat between her legs sent a jolt straight to his cock and all resolve was surrendered. He came crashing down on top of her, claiming her mouth and body with his masterful touch. He grabbed a handful of Charlee's hair and yanked her head to the side, raking his fangs up her neck. He shoved his hand down the front of her panties, feeling her wet heat, before he ripped them off, needing to feel more. *Fuck!*

He forced her legs open wider with his knee.

"RC," she moaned.

God, the sounds she was making were calling out the beast. He was going to explode. He gripped her hair harder while he claimed her lips with a fierce hunger.

"RC." Charlee struggled to talk.

"That's right, baby, keep saying my name."

"RC, you're…"

"Fucking amazing? I know."

Charlie slapped him; the sting doused the flames. He sat up, surprised by her reaction. "What the…?"

"You were hurting me."

Her lips were tinged red. Twin trails of blood were smeared down her neck. "Fuck. I'm…" He should be nowhere near Charlee. He jumped off the truck bed, then faced her. "I'm sorry." He back-stepped, trying to create distance, until he collided with the magnolia tree behind him.

"RC." Charlee sat up. "I'm fine."

"No, no." He shoved his hands through his hair. "It's not fine. I can't be trusted around you, Charlee girl. Things have changed and we're going to have to accept it."

Charlee climbed over the tailgate and jumped down. "I do accept it. Can't you see? We need time to get this right." Charlee walked over to him and reached for his hand, but he pulled away and strode to the truck with the worst case of blue balls he'd ever felt.

"Get in the truck. I'm taking you home."

She didn't budge.

"I said get in the truck."

"No."

"If you don't get in the truck, I'll pick your ass up and put you in it."

Charlee arched a brow. "Then do it."

Oh, for fuck's sake. What kind of a game was she playing? *Doesn't she know she's playing with wildfire?* RC strode back to the tree and was welcomed by Charlee's dress being thrown at him. He stopped dead in his tracks when her naked body came into view.

"I'm not going anywhere until you finish what you started," Charlee demanded.

She stood with her hands on her hips. Nothing could rival how beautiful her naked silhouette looked in the moonlight, but that beauty came with a whole lot of stubborn. RC's jaw ticked as he glared at her.

"Don't you dare do this to us. I'm willing and able to handle any kind of crazy going on in your head. I trust you. Why can't you trust me?"

"Charlee." He took a step closer. "It's not you. It's me. I've already lost control. What if you can't stop me? I'd die if I hurt you."

"But you *did* stop. If you trust me, then let me handle this." She kissed him, then went to the truck. She spread the blanket on the ground, then encouraged him to lie down. "Trust me," she whispered.

He couldn't say no. He owed her so much. And though he had doubts, nothing could stop this, nothing.

Charlee climbed on top of him, working the snaps on his button-fly while he kicked off his boots. She slipped his Wranglers off and there were no barriers left between them.

With feather-light strokes, she ran her fingers across his chest. Her touch soothed him, beating back the chaos inside him. It was working.

"Are you okay?" she asked.

"Mm-hm."

"Good. Ready for more?"

"Yes, ma'am."

She gripped his cock, sliding her hand up and down with an even, steady motion, stirring his need back to life. He reached down and grabbed her hand. "I need you now, baby." He pushed her hand from his cock and took it into his own hand, sliding it down and over her clit to the wet heat of her entrance. She slid down his length, inch by tantalizing inch until he was buried deep. "Aah, fuck!" he hissed. He held her there for a moment, feeling her stretch around him.

She felt so good sliding up and down his dick. He needed more. He grabbed her ass and picked up the pace, thrusting into her.

"Uh, uh. Slow and easy, cowboy."

Slow and easy? He wanted her to ride him like a buckin' bull. In time he'd have her his way, but for now she was in control. Barely.

They found their rhythm. RC's orgasm was coming on strong. His fangs descended and that instinctual urge to conquer surged through him again. He freaked and gripped Charlee's hips to move her off of him.

As if she understood his fears, Charlee tilted his chin up and looked him in the eyes. "Stay with me."

With his focus on her, he let go, allowing himself to enjoy the mind-blowing sensations she was giving him. But he wanted her to feel the same. He reached between her legs and rubbed her clit while he pumped deeper inside her. She moaned in his ear, which made him feel like a devil.

"Oh God, RC."

"Come with me, baby," he whispered through gritted teeth, the last thread of his control about to snap the fuck in half.

Her muscles tightened around his cock. He had her right where he wanted her. As his orgasm intensified, he stroked her faster, sending her over the edge at the same time. She buried her head in the crook of his neck and nipped him. He cupped her ass with both hands, holding on as a wave of electric heat sparked through him. Stars bust behind his eyes, brighter than he'd ever seen when he'd been human. He'd done it! He'd just made love to his Charlee girl and he hadn't killed her. Life couldn't get much better than that.

He waited for Charlee to catch her breath. If this was how slow and easy felt, he couldn't wait for all-out down and dirty. He looked down at her and kissed her shoulder. "Hey, you okay?"

She nodded. "That was incredible."

"Yeah, it was." He took her hand in his. "You want to do it again?" He kissed her fingers and wiggled his brows, his cock already hard again. This was a vamp benefit he could get used to.

Charlee giggled.

A few minutes ticked by. He held her close, threading his fingers through her soft hair. Her long legs were draped across his, her hand resting on his chest. He marveled at how good it felt to have her breasts pressed against his body, to remember everything about her. If he had the power to stop time and stay this way forever, he'd do it in a heartbeat. But time didn't exist anymore; he was an immortal. The innocence of their relationship had been stolen by his untimely death and darkness. She might accept him, but his world would reject her.

Underground Diablo was no place for a human. During his training on the streets, he saw things he wished he could unsee. Vampires ran freely. It was their domain, and they behaved badly. The human blood slave trade was a dirty business and profitable for the bloodsuckers. A vamp takes what a vamp wants. It turned his stomach.

If he took Charlee underground, he'd be sending her to her death.

He detested the thought of taking her away from everything that made her human. He was now the property of Hell's Cowboys, a duty he had accepted and lived by. He served his kind, and dished out justice with the crack of his whip.

Here he was again, bound to break Charlee's heart. He didn't see any other way. He was devoted to the underworld and she had to live where the sun touched her skin. Finding a way to break the bad news wouldn't be easy, especially when she started to ask questions.

But tonight, he would live in his dream world and love his Charlee girl until she was branded into his skin like a tattoo.

Chapter Eleven

After making up for lost time, several times over, breakfast was non-negotiable, but a cupcake request wasn't what Charlee had in mind. Eggs and bacon was more like it. However, she couldn't deny her cowboy his one special wish, strawberry shortcake cupcakes. The ones where she would hide a plump berry in the yellow cake and top it off with a swirl of whip cream. She hadn't made these tasty treats in a long time. Hopefully, she remembered the recipe.

She pulled on her favorite worn blue jeans and slipped on a pink tee, then tied her just-had-mind-blowing-sex hair up into a lazy bun. "Are you sure you want cupcakes for breakfast?" She walked back to the bed where RC was lying on his back with a watchful eye on her.

Her gaze roamed down his muscled chest. Just then it hit her; he had changed so much. He'd always stayed toned, but now his physique was enhanced. Pure, raw male strength bled from every pore, from every fiber of his new body. And those deep amber eyes were breathtaking. The familiarity was still there, but something dark lurked behind them. And that was most definitely not the RC she had known.

The sun barely peeked over the horizon, dimly lighting her bedroom. She looked down at RC. Straight white teeth smiled back at her. *RC has fangs?*

He sat up. "What's wrong, baby?"

"Nothing." She shook free from her thoughts. "I can't believe you're alive and in my bed." She caressed his cheek.

"I'm as alive as I'm going to be." He covered her hand, then kissed her palm. "So, are you coming back to bed, or cooking?" He tried to pull her into bed.

Charlee gave him a little shove and he fell back against the pillows. "Whoa there cowboy. This filly needs food," she laughed. "Plus, you have me craving strawberries."

RC folded his hands behind his head. "Have it your way. Come and get me when you're done."

Charlee retrieved one of the throw pillows from the floor and flung it at him, hitting his chest.

RC sat up. "What was that for?"

Charlee grinned. "Just because."

Before he had a chance to retaliate, she ran out of the bedroom, closing the door behind her.

Charlee couldn't stop smiling as she reached the kitchen and collected measuring cups and spoons from a drawer. She went to the pantry and gathered the ingredients to make the cupcakes. With her arms full, she set the items down on the counter, then opened the refrigerator for the eggs and strawberries.

Since Gran had passed, she hadn't baked often, so this was a rare treat. She cracked an egg over the bowl and then whisked in some vanilla extract. There were a lot of things she used to enjoy but had pushed aside. Now she spent most of her time working so she didn't lose the ranch.

She measured out the flour and dumped it into the sifter. Maybe Mace was right. Maybe it was time to live for herself and sell the ranch. With what he was offering, she could buy another house and still have money left over to go back to college. It was a no brainer. She wouldn't have to go back to stripping or worry about the bank foreclosing on her home. She could feel the stress being lifted from her shoulders as she considered being debt free.

All she had to do was accept his offer.

Some things are too good to be true. Why did Mace want her ranch so desperately that he was willing to pay triple the market value? Her instincts warned her that his money didn't come without strings attached.

She looked around the kitchen. There was so much updating to be done. The cabinets dated back to the 1920s when her great-granddad and grandma had bought the place. Some of the cabinet doors were falling off their hinges and creaked so bad that she had removed the ones above the stove, leaving open shelves. To keep the kitchen looking nice, she sewed some curtains do-it-yourself style to cover the cabinets housing her kitchen gadgets.

It was a quick fix. Even though Gran kept a tidy house, it was time for a kitchen makeover. And that wasn't going to happen any time soon on her limited funds.

She poured the batter into a cupcake pan, filling the white paper cups a quarter of an inch from the top, then burying a strawberry in each cupcake.

This was her home. Losing it meant letting go of a piece of herself. The house with all its flaws represented everything she loved the most. The cattle had been sold off long ago and she'd considered renting out a couple acres for grazing, but local ranchers were financially pressed as well, leaving most no option but to sell their land.

After popping the pan into the oven, Charlee licked the batter off the mixer beater.

"God." She closed her eyes. "This tastes like heaven."

Leaning her hip against the counter, she studied the living room, reminiscing. It was just as Gran had left it; antique plates and tea pots decorated the shelves, collecting dust she hadn't had time to clean. Framed pictures of distant memories were on display on the mantel above the fireplace. She set the beater down on the counter and walked into the living room. Gran had loved photos. Charlee picked up a gold frame and dusted it off with her shirt. She chuckled. It was a shot of her in her high school cheerleading uniform with big poufy hair and skinny legs. Such a time of innocence.

She replaced the frame and another photograph caught her attention. One of RC pushing her on a swing hanging from one of the oak trees in her backyard. She traced his smiling face with her finger—a somber feeling crept in. They had been so happy back then. Could they find happiness again? She tried to push his current circumstances to the back of her mind. It didn't matter how drastically his world had changed. Could love bridge the gap between them?

God, she hoped so.

Charlee stepped back from the mantel, still admiring the family photos. One particular image of Gran and Pop Pop stared back at her. Every wrinkle that etched their faces told a story of how devoted they had been. They built this home out of love. As if the gray cloud had lifted, Charlee's answers unfolded right before her. She just hoped she could weather the storm long enough to build a new life. That new life with RC started as soon as he came down for breakfast. She was willing to do whatever it took to be with the man she loved.

Someone knocked on the front door and she rushed to the window. A black limousine with tinted windows was parked out front. *What is Mace doing here?* Quickly, she took down her hair and finger-combed the strands into submission. *What could he possibly want?*

She opened the door. Two hooded men pushed their way inside. Before she could scream, one of them covered her mouth with a damp cloth. She kicked and struggled, but the man behind her held on tight. She gave in to the sweet, chemical smell on the cloth and everything went black.

Chapter Twelve

Kit slammed his coffee cup into the automatic java cave and pushed the strong setting until the damn button almost broke. He'd been sucking down coffee all night like it was water. The lead he was piecing together had run straight to Mace Wrathmore, aka a dhampir's worst nightmare. The bloodsuckers back at the D&D were working for the king of the underground, but what he couldn't figure out was why.

The club was above ground, and until a few days ago, a safe place for half-breeds to unwind. He knew Val and Vin wouldn't tip off the enemy; they were allies. Well, as close as one could be with demons. So, how had those bastards known when they would be at the club?

That was the question bogging down this whole operation and pissing him off. What were the vampires up to? He tapped his index finger on the table while considering his dilemma.

With Wrathmore having announced a hefty bounty on a half-breed's head, someone could have tipped them off. It was a real possibility. But, who? Something was off, he could feel it. The gunmen weren't discreet. In fact, all out, balls-to-the-wall shooting in a busy place seemed out of character for the vampires the Cowboys usually dealt with. There was more to this mystery.

Kit mentally retraced that night's events. The shots had come from upstairs first, then chaos had broken out. This had to be a botched hit. Kit scratched the stubble on his chin. "Shit!" He slammed his fist on the table, sending his cup sailing to the floor. He was right back at the beginning. Who were these assholes after?

Forgetting about his coffee, Kit strode back behind his command station and then plopped down in his office chair, leaning back until the damn thing almost cracked in two. He shoved his hands through his sandy brown hair. Usually he shined under pressure, calm as a horse grazing in a pasture, but frustration had gotten the best of him. He needed to clear his mind.

It occurred to him that two hours had passed since he'd checked on RC's human. Like he had time to babysit. In a frustrated huff, Kit wheeled in closer to a set of computer monitors, then rewound the camera footage back a few hours. He then forwarded through the black and gray images of the previous night. He leaned in and recognized a familiar truck pulling into Charlee's driveway.

"What the hell? RC?" They were on lockdown. "Sly fuck." Kit continued searching through the footage. Looked as if the lovers reconciled as he watched RC carry Charlee over the threshold, then shoot the camera a warming middle finger greeting.

Everything seemed in place over in loversville. He bet the lovebirds were chirping all night long. Kit shook his head, refusing to allow himself to envy RC. The one female he'd dared to love had ripped him to shreds inside and feasted on his heart. *No thank you, I'll pass on the love-stricken fool card.*

With thirty minutes left on the surveillance tape, Kit had seen enough and was about to pick up where he left off on the bloodsuckers, when an image blipped off and on the screen.

"No, don't tell me I need another software update." Kit punched keys with fast determination to fix the blasted glitch. Another blip. He sobered and drew closer to the monitor. Two men dressed in black, hooded faces...vampires? Nah, the sun was up. He checked his watch. The sun had just peeked...no, it was too risky. He froze as he watched one of the men carry Charlee's limp body into the limo. "Sweet Lilith! They've got Charlee!" Kit jumped out of the chair. "Where's RC?"

Pulling out his cell, he speed-dialed RC. "Come on, pick up, you bastard." He paced. "Fuck, voicemail."

Kit redialed as he grabbed his hat and rushed out of the lab. He raced down the hall to the elevator, the door slid open, and he strode in. Since the Cowboys were on lockdown, he knew Clay would be deep into his morning routine and easy to find. "Shit, voicemail again."

The doors hissed open, and like a caged animal being freed, Kit hit the hallway running, pressing redial on his cell. It all made sense now. Those bloodsuckers weren't after the Cowboys; they were after Charlee. And now, possibly RC.

He busted down the door, entering the compound out of breath.

Tibbs shot up from the couch with a pistol aimed at Kit's head. "Fuck, man. I almost pulled the trigger."

"Where's Clay? We have a situation," Kit said, breathing heavy from the adrenaline rush.

"What in damnation?" Clay came out of his room and passed the shattered door. "Kit?"

"Clay, we have a situation. RC's human has been abducted by the same bloodsuckers from the club. I just put the pieces together. They weren't after us. They were after Charlee."

All the color washed from Clay's face. "Where's RC?"

Tibbs coughed.

"The surveillance last showed him at Charlee's house and that was over…" He looked at his watch, "Eleven hours ago. And I can't reach him on his cell."

Clay glared at Tibbs. "He broke lockdown?"

"Look, before you go jumpin' my shit," Tibbs said, "I gave him his keys. He was driving me crazy, sulking. He needed his woman."

"Do we have a lead on Charlee?" Clay asked.

"No—wait," Kit said.

If the vampires at the club were behind her abduction, he'd know. Before he'd let the attacker go, he'd injected him with a GPS microchip. The last few days Kit had been following the man, and up until now it had been a bust. Kit ran into his room and grabbed his laptop, popping it open in record time. Some fast typing and a few seconds later, bingo, he had the subject pinned above ground. "Got it. They're headed west on Bio Hazard Road."

"That's in the middle of the desert," Tibbs said.

Irritated, Clay grabbed his keys and set the plan in motion. "Kit, keep tabs on the suspect. Tibbs, keep trying to reach RC. We're going after Charlee. And Kit."

"Yeah, Hoss?"

"I want to know every detail on the way, understood?"

Kit nodded. *Shit, they weren't dealing with vamps.*

***

RC immersed himself beneath the spray. Only a cold shower could ease the tension between his legs. When he'd made Charlee the offer to come back to bed, he'd hoped she would take it. He loved her strawberry cupcakes, but he'd much rather bury himself in her cupcake. After a few minutes of tossing and turning with his dick standing at full attention, he did what any sexed-up male with no other options would do, and hit the shower.

Water streamed off his broad back and chest, intensifying the fiery trails Charlee had left behind with her nails. He leaned back, wetting his hair, then scrubbed his face. Just the thought of her hands on his body sent him into a lustful frenzy, which wasn't helping his hard-on predicament. He grabbed the soap and lathered his chest. He couldn't believe how lucky he was to have her. He saw it in her eyes and felt it in her touch; she'd accepted him for who he'd become.

His hands moved down his abdomen. Yep, he was hard as a rock with Charlee's ass on his mind. He gripped his cock and imagined his girl kneeling in front of him with that sexy smirk of hers, ready to take him into her beautiful mouth. *Fuck!* He leaned forward, resting his arm on the cold tiled wall while his other hand stroked his length, sliding up and down until he felt the pressure of his release. He threw his head back and sucked in a breath. It didn't take much effort; his orgasm hit him like a blast.

He stood there for a moment, spent, and gathered his breath. Suddenly, the sweet aroma of yellow cake baking in the oven turned foul. It was burning. *What's going on? Charlee never burns her cakes.*

Shutting off the water, RC grabbed a towel and wrapped it around his waist, then stepped out of the shower. He padded across her bedroom and into the hallway. "Charlee girl, everything all right?"

When there was no reply, worry set in and he raced downstairs, holding his towel in place. "Charlee!" He'd hung his bull rope at the end of the stairs last night. Good thing, because something was telling him he was going to need it.

With his rope in hand and ready to snap, RC rounded the corner to the kitchen. Smoke billowed from the oven, and Charlee was nowhere in sight. Throwing the glowing rope on the counter, RC strode over to the oven, opened it, reached in, and then grabbed the cupcake pan. "Fuck!" He threw the hot pan in the sink and then opened the window above so the smoke could escape.

A vibrating noise drew his attention to the kitchen table, where his cellphone lay. *God, please let it be Charlee!*

He raced over to the table and snatched up his phone. "Hello, Charlee?"

"Sweet cheeks!"

"Fuck you, Tibbs. What do you want? I don't have time for games."

RC heard Tibbs yell to someone that he had reached him.

"Hey." Tibbs returned to the phone. "Where are you?"

RC shoved his hands through his wet hair. "I'm here at Charlee's. I just got out of the shower and came downstairs to find her gone."

"Listen, We're following Kit's lead. He saw two men on surveillance footage abducting Charlee from her home early this morning."

"Christ!"

"He believes the abductors are the same assholes who attacked the club. They were after Charlee."

"Are you sure?"

"If Kit believes so. I'd follow that bastard into the bowels of hell."

"He better be right. I swear if anything happens to her..." RC couldn't allow himself to think about such tragedy.

"They're heading down Bio Hazard Road. We're about twenty minutes behind."

Shit! "I'm on my way." RC slammed his cell down on the table and took the stairs two at a time to the bedroom to dress. If those fuckers hurt Charlee, he'd rip them limb-from-limb.

In a flash, he was dressed and out the door. Making sure his Aviators were securely protecting his eyes, he headed to his truck and snapped his rope, warming it up. Rage pumped through his body and begged to be released. Never before had such anger pulsed through him. In a way, it scared him, for he had no control over it. "Charlee girl, I'm coming."

Chapter Thirteen

Mace sat cross-legged in the passenger seat of a broken-down RV in the middle of the desert, studying his latest victim's unconscious body that was duct taped to the driver's seat. He checked his watch; time was running out. In less than thirty minutes, the sun's rays would pierce through his UV protective clothing and fry him extra crispy.

He was taking a huge, life-threatening risk being in this barren wasteland with its deadly heat and sunlight. Another failed plan wasn't an option. He had to micromanage this job. Much was riding on it. Nothing was going to stop him from getting what he wanted.

The skin under his collar began to itch. Shit, he hated to sweat. It was a sign of weakness on so many levels.

Mace kicked the driver's seat, trying to speed up the wakey-wakey process. To his amusement, the victim moaned and struggled to steady her head. It really was a shame he had to resort to such harsh measures; it was not like he got off on murder. He saw it merely as removing a threat.

There was a time when he'd felt remorse for his sins, when he gave a rat's ass about others, but that was long ago. Love had scarred him, teaching him two valuable lessons. One; trust no one, especially a female. And two;

never leave a loaded .45 on your nightstand, you'll wake up in the morning with an awful headache.

No, there was no room for remorse. The human had to go. Land development contractors were outbidding each other left and right, salivating at Mace's plans for the rural area. Resources in the city were thinning and he needed to branch out. It was the perfect place to develop a new community.

The humans believed Mace when he promised to create jobs and build affordable housing communities. And yes, that was exactly what he intended to do, yet his intentions were different.

This project was another area for him to control and vampires to feed off the sin that always came with the package deal. It was a holding area for humans, a guaranteed food source for the vampires. His livelihood depended on this deal. It solidified his authority above ground. Power was his lover now; its hunger—owning Diablo. Eradicating the half-breeds and vampire fuck-ups along the way, was icing on the cake.

His victim came to and thrashed against the tape binding her hands, feet, and mouth. Fear. It was a human emotion, one he despised. And mortals reeked of it. Mace found it amusing to watch terror streak across her face, knowing she was going to die. "Nice for you to join me, Ms. Brysen," he said.

Charlee moaned.

"What's that?" Mace cupped his hand next to his ear and leaned in. "I don't understand what you're saying."

Tears ran down her dirty cheeks.

"Oh, you want to know why you're in the desert taped to the driver's seat of an RV? Well, Ms. Brysen, it's rather simple. I always get what I want." Mace slipped behind the driver's seat and freed one of her hands.

He gazed at her over his sunglasses. "I'm really sorry we didn't reach an agreement."

He grabbed her hand, fixated on her index finger, then sucked it into his mouth. He punctured the tip with his fangs, tasting her blood. *Fuck!* His eyes rolled back in his head. "You taste divine." Then he flipped her hand over and traced the veins in her wrist, traveling up her arm. "You would've made a perfect blood slave."

He reached inside his suit pocket and retrieved the deed to her ranch. Laying the agreement across his lap, he pressed her bloody finger along the signature line. "Vampire law or human law, it doesn't matter. One way or another, I will have your land."

He pinched her finger, pooling more blood at the tip, then slowly rolled it across his tongue, reveling in her essences.

His cock hardened as the red sweetness reached the back of his throat, causing him to suck harder. Centuries old and he'd never tasted blood like this before. How much sweeter would it be if he was fucking her senseless right now, savoring every last drop at the same time? How much time did he have left with her? His smoldering skin told him his time was up.

Regaining his composure, he released Charlee's hand, then kneeled to activate the device around her ankle. When he straightened, he met her pleading face. The sound of her frantic heartbeat caused him to stroke her cheek. "If you would've said yes... now, you have to disappear. Nothing personal; it's business."

He exited through the passenger side, then stuck his head back inside. "Old Bessy here is loaded with explosives. Go ahead, look behind you." Mace pointed to the back where rows of brown square bags were stacked.

Charlee looked behind her then met Mace's stare, pleading through the duct tape across her mouth.

"I just activated your ankle detonator. If you should escape the restraints, you won't be going far. I'm sure your knight in cowboy boots will come and try to save you. The device will activate a timer as soon as you leave, giving you seconds before the explosives ignite. You and your half-breed fuck will die." He tapped his chin. "You know, I've always been really good at multitasking.

"Ms. Brysen, like I said before, I always get what I want. With you gone, nothing will stop me." Mace slammed the door before he could change his mind and make her his slave.

After he climbed into the limo, he collapsed from exhaustion. His skin blistered beneath his clothes.

"Crawley, take me home," he whispered.

"Yes, sir."

He closed his eyes as he loosened his tie. Almost dying because of a human ranked right up there with vampire-gone-crazy. At least the job was done and he could move on.

***

RC caught up with Clay, Tibbs, and Kit in record time, following them down Bio Hazard Road behind the plumes of dust that his truck was kicking up. But he didn't need to use his sight to get to Charlee. He felt her as if she pulsed through the air.

"What the hell? Why is Clay stopping?"

RC slammed on his brakes, coming to an abrupt stop, barely missing Clay's bumper. As the dust cleared, five men clothed in black, were standing in front of a gray Bentley Flying Spur. Shoulder-to-shoulder, they were set up like a road block.

RC opened his door, then paused. Charlee wasn't here. Anger raged through him, knowing these cockbags had laid a hand on his girl.

Slamming the door, RC shifted into reverse, then aimed his truck perfectly at the driver's side of the fucker's car. He revved the engine, sending out a warning. The men didn't budge, calling his bluff.

"Alright then." RC punched the gas, back tires spinning like hell on wheels. He went full throttle, racing toward the barrier.

The men scattered in every direction as he crashed his truck into the Bentley.

RC's head bounced off the steering wheel. The blow didn't affect him; in fact, it pissed him off, adding fuel to the fire. He shouldered the door open and stepped out with his bull rope in hand.

Clay, Tibbs and Kit joined him.

"What the fuck are you doing?" Clay yelled.

"Raisin' hell!" RC answered, snapping his bull rope.

"Hell yeah." Tibbs smiled, holding two glowing daggers in each hand, itching to draw blood.

Like an old western faceoff, both sides formed a line and strode toward each other anticipating the fight, daring someone to make the first move. With confident strides, the Cowboys primed their weapons, ready to send these demons back to hell. RC could smell the fear in one particular man—the one in the middle squirming under his gaze. He'd taken Charlee.

RC spun his rope into a lasso, waiting to strike. He stalked the bastard, causing him to back-step like a coward. *This fuck is going down.*

In an attempt to save his comrade, one of the bastards charged RC. All hell broke loose as the Cowboys advanced the attack.

Lightning fast, RC unleashed his rope, looping it around the attacker's neck like a noose. He ripped the man's head clean from his body with one hard yank, sending the beast to the ground. The head rolled toward the coward who now stood stunned. The bastard took one look at RC, then tucked tail and ran.

Ah, the chase was on.

With a calm, frightening stride, he tracked the fleeing fool, twirling another lasso. Once he locked in on the target, he unleashed the rope and captured him. Quickly he tightened the slack, binding the bastard's arms to his side. He reeled in his prize, winding the excess rope around his arm. He pulled the asshole closer, then cold-cocked him in the face. "Where's Charlee?" he asked.

"Fuck you!" The demon snarled. "I'm not going to tell you anything."

RC tugged on the rope, coiling it tighter around the demon, cutting into his hide. He'd force the bastard to talk. "I won't ask you again. Where's Charlee?"

RC's brothers joined him. He watched with intense interest as Tibbs slashed and stabbed with his daggers, Kit demonstrated his mastery of martial arts, and Clay delivered an old-fashioned ass beating. None of them broke a sweat.

In that moment, as RC eyed the injured demons on the ground, he realized how lucky he was to be a part of this team.

"Let's keep this one alive," Clay said. "Roman will want to interrogate him."

"Fine. I'm going after Charlee." Wasting no time, RC strode to his truck. Looking out his dusty windshield, he searched the open desert for some sign of his girl. She was close, he could feel it.

"Alright, sweet cheeks, let's go get her." Tibbs jumped into the passenger side.

Surprised, RC looked at him.

"What? You think you're alone? We haven't come this far to fail," Tibbs said.

RC was speechless. These cowboys were pulling together to help him find Charlee. They were putting their lives on the line for him. He started the truck and drove back down Bio Hazard Road, where he felt Charlee's essence the strongest.

He glanced out his rearview mirror and noticed Clay's truck following. He shook his head. Something had shifted in his relationship with the Cowboys. He didn't know when it happened or if it had always been there. From this moment on, he'd accept that he wasn't a lone wolf. The same assholes he'd resisted, now had his back. They cared about Charlee, and for that, he'd forever be indebted.

With Charlee in danger, RC couldn't waste any more time. He pushed the Ford beyond its ability. Judging by the knocking noise coming from the engine, he'd be lucky if he made it in time.

The electricity running through his veins pulsed faster the closer he came to Charlee. Off in the distance, he noticed a RV. Taking a hard right, he drove off the road.

"She's there." He pointed to the vehicle.

He slammed into park, then hit the ground running, ripping the camper door off its hinges. "Charlee!"

Whimpers sounded from the front. *Holy shit!* He raced to Charlee and removed the tape from her mouth. "Charlee girl, everything will be all right. I'm here."

"No, Russel," she said through labored breaths. "You have to leave. It's a trap."

"Who did this to you?" RC continued removing the bindings.

At that moment, Tibbs opened the back of the RV. "Whoa!! That's a lot of boom?"

RC glanced back and slowly stood as he spotted the brown sacks. "What the…"

"Yep, you're looking at I'd say at least eight hundred pounds of explosives. Enough to blow us into nonexistence," Tibbs said.

Charlee stood, holding her stomach and trembling. A mixture of sweat and tears streaked her face. He wasn't sure how to outrun this fireball, which terrified RC to the bone. Yet he couldn't show it. He had to be strong for Charlee, because she was on the verge of a meltdown.

He cupped her face, thumbing away the tears. "We're in this together. I'll get us out of here. I swear."

Charlee shook her head and looked back at the explosives.

"Look at me, sweetheart." RC locked eyes with her. "I'm getting us out of here. Alive. Do you understand me?"

Chapter Fourteen

Charlee tried to find comfort in RC. She wanted to believe there was a way out of this mess. But how? If she took one step off the RV, the detonator would trigger the explosives. Even if she had the courage to run, she wouldn't have enough time to outrun the danger.

Charlee stepped into RC's embrace, feeling the weight of her destiny in the anklet.

"Charlee girl, we need to find the detonator. Do you know where it is?"

She looked up at him. "It's around my ankle. If I leave the RV, it will activate the timer. We'll have seconds before the bomb will go off." She paused, thinking back to what Mace had told her. *That's it!* If she could remove the detonator, then she could leave.

She took a step back as hope flooded over her. "We need to remove the anklet."

"Here, sit down and I'll try," RC said.

She sat in the driver's seat and reached down, tugging at the strap on the device.

"Whoa," RC warned. "We don't want to upset this little guy. Let me try."

RC carefully searched for a hinge or clasp to pry it apart. He worked at the seam with no luck. "Who did this to you?" he ground out.

She didn't know where to start. "Mace Wrathmore."

"Damn, woman, you should choose your friends more wisely." Tibbs stepped into the RV, looking over RC's shoulder.

"Do you mind? I'm kinda busy here," RC lashed out.

"Oh, you're not going to remove that until the timer starts," Tibbs said.

"What do you mean?"

Tibbs bent down and observed the blinking metal. "The clasps on this bad boy won't open until the timer is detonated. And from what I can see, this looks like you got about five seconds to high-tail it out of here before the boom."

"Five seconds?" Charlee asked.

"Yep."

RC stood and removed his hat, wiping the sweat from his forehead.

Charlee glanced down at the ring of red lights pulsing around her ankle. "Do you know how to disarm it?"

"There's no kill switch," Tibbs said.

"What do you mean, no kill switch? Isn't there a wire we can snip?" RC placed his hand on Charlee's shoulder. "There has to be a way out."

Tibbs straightened, adjusting his mirror-lensed shades. "Whoever rigged this knew what they were doing. I only see one way out of here."

RC glared at him. "Which is?"

"I hope you have your running shoes on."

As the cowboys deliberated an escape, Charlee saw the horror written on their faces. Their words faded as she drifted into numbness, knowing she was going to die. This was it. She had to make a choice. Either RC and her left together, jeopardizing both of their lives or she'd stay and risk her own. She'd got herself into this mess. If she'd only given Mace what he wanted, she wouldn't be here.

She sat and her shoulders slumped. Tears rolled down her face as she stared at the anklet. There was only one way out, and she wasn't going to let RC die because of her stupid mistake.

***

RC glanced over Tibbs's shoulder and saw Charlee fading. "Hey, give us a sec."

"No problem, man." Tibbs gave him a sorrowful nod and left the RV.

Wiping his sweaty palms down his Wranglers, RC approached Charlee. "Hey."

She looked defeated and RC's heart broke. They were going to make it out. He'd see to it.

"Listen." He knelt down on one knee and took her hands in his. "I know we haven't had time to talk about my crazy life, the change and all. But I do come with benefits." He saw the corner of Charlee's lips lift in a half-smile.

"Oh yeah." She sniffled. "Like what, teleportation?"

RC chuckled. "No, I wish. It would sure make our situation a lot better, wouldn't it?"

"I'm so sorry that I brought you into this mess."

"Charlee, what are you not telling me?"

"You know the date I went on with Mace Wrathmore?"

RC gritted his teeth. "Yes."

"He wanted to buy my ranch, and since I turned him down, this is his retaliation. He's a vampire, RC. Before he left, he…" She swallowed hard. "He forced me to sign my ranch over to him." She hung her head. "I've lost everything."

"Hey." He lifted her chin. "You're lucky he left you alive. Mace Wrathmore is a very evil, powerful vampire. Your ranch must be extremely important for him to risk his life coming out in the sun."

Charlee squeezed his hand. "He said he wants to kill you."

"That bastard wants to dispose of all dhampirs. Like I said, he's dangerous and you're lucky to be alive."

"Yeah, but not for long."

"Hey, you're the strongest woman I know, a fighter. Plus, I'm here now."

"So, what are these benefits of yours?"

"I can run really fast. There's no doubt we can outrun the blast. It's the shockwave we'll have to be careful of."

"So, you're saying we're going to make a run for it?"

"Yes, ma'am."

"I can't. If anything happens to you—"

"It won't. I'm immortal. The explosion may ring my bell a little, but it won't kill me. In fact, I can protect you from the blast."

Charlee shook her head. "I don't know."

"Hey, you've seen what I can do in eight seconds." He winked. "Trust me. I can do a whole lot more than that now."

RC waited for what seemed like an eternity for her to respond. He wasn't going to leave without her. He'd stay until she agreed with the plan. And if she didn't, he'd fling her over his shoulder, giving her no choice.

"Okay," she whispered. "I trust you with all of my heart."

RC smiled. "That's my Charlee girl." He stood, taking her with him. "Let's get out of here."

They stopped abruptly at the side door. "Tibbs!" RC called.

"Yeah, boss?"

"Get the trucks in place. We're coming out."

"Roger that." Tibbs took off toward the trucks and motioned for Clay to follow.

RC waited until the pickups were parked. He surveyed the area, making sure his plan was solid. All he had to do was make it to the trucks; from that point on, they were home free. *Five seconds.* Judging by the amount of explosives packed in the rear of the RV, the aftershock would be huge. Miles of terrain would be torn up, not to mention all the flying debris. God, he hoped he was making the right decision.

He turned to Charlee. "Are you ready?"

She stared out into the desert, then nodded.

"Okay. I'll step out of the RV first, then you'll jump into my arms. Leave the rest to me. I'll take care of it." He gave her a reassuring grin.

He hit the ground with a thud. He took Charlee's hand. "Ready, Charlee girl?"

Without hesitation, he scooped Charlee into his arms. As soon as she left the RV, the detonator flashed green and flew off her ankle. She buried her head into his neck and held on tight. In a flash, he was off and running, praying every step of the way.

They were halfway there, only seconds remaining on the clock. He pumped his legs faster, pushing himself harder and harder. He held the whole world in his arms; he'd make it.

They were within a foot of the safe zone when RC felt the shift. He dared to look behind him, knowing what was about to take place. His vampire side kicked in, and in slow motion, he saw the RV glow bright from the inside, then expand, exploding into a flaming inferno. Smoke and fire plumed like a mushroom, then spread

133

over the desert, sending fiery debris in every direction. The boom was deafening.

Fuck! The earth tremored. The shockwave was coming straight for them, racing fifteen times as fast as a speeding bullet. There was no time to waste, he had to protect her. Thankful for his vampire speed and quick reflexes, he stopped, dropped, and covered Charlee with his body just as the flames flashed over them. He felt the heat and prayed they would be spared the full effect of the shockwave.

The dust settled and RC slowly uncovered Charlee. Relief washed over him as he heard her heart still beating and felt her breathing beneath him. He brushed her hair away from her face. "Charlee girl, we made it."

Charlee coughed up blood. "Charlee?" He sat back on his heels. "No. No. Fuck no!"

A piece of twisted metal protruded from her stomach, her clothes were covered in blood. She tried to pull it out, but RC stopped her. She looked down at her mangled body. "Oh, God, RC."

The object was embedded deep, and if he pulled it out, she could very well bleed to death. "Shhh. Leave it. You're going to be fine."

Clay, Kit and Tibbs ran to RC's side.

"Christ!" Clay swore.

"She needs Selene. ASAP," Kit said. "I'll call ahead so she can get ready."

"I'll go get the truck." Tibbs ran back toward the pickups.

In a flash, Tibbs was back with the truck and opened the passenger door.

RC picked Charlee up, careful not to disturb the wound. "Don't worry about a thing, darlin'. I got you." He slid into the truck, and Tibbs hauled ass back to the compound.

RC monitored her breathing; she was fading. "Tibbs, can you go any faster?"

"I'm going as fast as your hunk of junk will allow." Tibbs looked over at Charlee. "She's lost a lot of blood."

"No shit," RC bit back.

"Give her your blood. It's not strong enough to heal her, but it will keep her stable until we get to Selene."

There was no thinking twice about it. His fangs dropped, he sliced his wrist, then hovered it above her lips. "Drink, Charlee girl. My blood can help you. It's one of those added benefits I have." He was trying to keep her thinking positive, and he'd die trying to keep her alive.

A part of him was ashamed of what he'd become when Charlee hesitated to take his wrist. Somehow, it hurt his vampire pride. But as soon as his blood entered her mouth, she clamped her lips around the slash and sucked.

"That's it." He caressed her head.

Tibbs turned right off the highway and onto a one lane, gravel road that wound behind a mountain, leading them into the main, underground tunnel. Bright lights whizzed past them as Tibbs accelerated. Taking a sharp left, they entered the Cowboys' parking garage. Tibbs whipped the Ford into its designated spot, jamming the thing in park.

Right behind them, Clay parked and removed their prisoner from his truck. "I need to take this asshole to Roman. I'll catch up with you." He shoved the bastard forward.

With Charlee in his arms, RC raced to the elevator where Tibbs and Kit were holding the door open. Within seconds, they were out and racing down the hallway to the infirmary. Selene greeted them at the door, ready to do what she did best—save lives.

"Lay her down, over here." Selene pointed

RC laid Charlee down on the hospital bed, but wouldn't leave her side. He brushed her hair away from her forehead and held her hand. "You're going to be just fine, Charlee girl." Her head rolled to the side. Christ, she was pale. She coughed up blood. "Selene! We're losing her!"

Selene slapped on her surgical gloves and walked over to Charlee, observing the piece of metal sticking out from her stomach.

Impatient, RC looked at Selene. "Well?"

Selene met his stare. "You're asking for a miracle, darlin'."

RC shook his head. This couldn't be happening. Charlee couldn't possibly be dying. He looked down at her chest slowly rising and falling. "Darlin' hang on..." His voice cracked. "Hang on for us." He leaned in and rested his forehead on hers.

Charlee's body went limp. He closed his eyes tight, wishing he'd wake from this nightmare. "No, Charlee girl."

"Someone, please, get him out of here," Selene demanded.

Tibbs walked up behind RC and squeezed his shoulder. "Come on. Let Selene do her job."

"I can't leave her."

"I know. But you're not helping Charlee by staying here."

RC stood and took a step back as he stared at Charlee's lifeless body. His mind numbed. His heart threatened to shatter. He couldn't fix this.

"Come on, RC." Tibbs ushered him to the door and Kit followed.

Hours passed as slow as molasses in January. RC paced outside the infirmary as he waited for Selene to give him an update. He wished he could trade places with Charlee. He even pleaded to God. Hell, he'd dance around a fire naked talking in tongues if he had to—anything to save her. It drove him insane that he couldn't do a damn thing. He was half vampire, yet not strong enough to give her life.

The door to the infirmary creaked open and Selene came out. RC froze. The sorrowful expression on the vampire's face read loud and clear. His knees buckled, but he regained his balance.

"Darlin', I did all I could. I've stitched the wound and stopped the bleeding."

137

"That's good, right?" RC held onto hope.

"She's lost a lot of blood—"

"Well, you're a vampire. Give her some of yours," RC demanded.

"She's too far gone. I'd have to give her a lot of blood, and that's too risky. She'll be lucky if she makes it through the night. I'm sorry, darlin'."

RC glared at Selene as he walked past her and into the infirmary.

"You're a piece of work," Kit addressed Selene.

"Look, I did all I could."

"Bullshit!"

Selene approached Kit. "What's your problem, Cowboy?"

"My problem is you have the ability to save that girl, yet won't do it. You're too much of a heartless bitch."

"Save her? Do you actually think turning her into a vampire is saving her?" She jabbed a finger at his chest. "I'm not turning her without her consent, and even if I had it, I still wouldn't do it. I know what it's like to live in the shadows. To hunt humans for their blood. It took a long time to learn to accept myself for what I've become. I wouldn't wish this life on anyone." Selene turned to walk away, but Kit grabbed her arm and spun her around.

"RC loves that girl. She's his life. It will destroy him if he loses her. If nothing else, turn her for love. Please," Kit pleaded.

Selene held his stare. "I don't play Goddess."

My Immortal Cowboy

Chapter Fifteen

Selene couldn't get away from Kit fast enough. She knew he was watching her walk away. On any other day, she'd give him an eyeful and exaggerate that country girl hitch in her step; give him a show he'd remember for a while. Nothing felt more satisfying than to see him sweat with desire. Fair play, considering he rattled her cage like no one else could.

She loved the way he hurt her when he lashed out, and she missed the misery when he wasn't around. It made her feel alive in some demented way.

She rounded the corner, out of Kit's sight, then rested her back against the cold, concrete wall. She fisted her hands and looked up at the ceiling, lightly banging her head. He'd crossed the line. The reason he wanted her to turn that girl was nothing more than a jab at her, reminding her of how she'd broken his heart.

"Turn her for love," Selene spat. Like this was supposed to soften her up or change her mind about their relationship. Yep, it was definitely a personal attack.

There was no denying the passion he brought out in her. Kit made her feel human again. Like secondhand smoke, she breathed him in, craving more. Yet she hated herself for wanting more than she deserved.

She was a cold-blooded vampire, damned to hell. Even though he was half vampire, there was a side she couldn't be a part of. At least that was what she told herself, because in reality there was always going to be one male who stood between them, and he was immortal. A threat that would never die. A threat she'd protect Kit from at all costs. Love was a high-stakes game in her world, and she didn't gamble.

She took her frustrations out on the concrete wall, banging her head harder, trying to get Kit out of her thoughts. But that was the problem; once he was in, he made himself at home. Sweet Lilith, it irked her how he got under her skin. But what bothered her the most, was how she *allowed* him to affect her. Why did he have to be so damn irresistible?

Heartless bitch. Kit's words cut her to the bone. Why did she care what he thought of her anyway? That girl wasn't her problem. *How dare he make such a request!* Turning a human wasn't taken lightly.

She had a precise purpose here and didn't need any distractions. Years ago, she'd joined Roman because she believed in his vision—all life matters, human, vampire, and dhampir.

All life matters.

Roman couldn't afford to lose a soldier over a broken heart. It was too dangerous for RC not to have his head in the game. They needed every cowboy mentally and physically prepared to beat Mace.

Shit. She had to save that girl.

Selene shoved off the wall and strode back to the infirmary. Her nerves got the best of her for a brief moment as she stood in the doorway watching RC sitting bedside, holding the girl's hand. This wasn't going to be easy. She was about to go against the one thing she vowed never to do.

Taking in a deep breath, she approached the bed, meeting RC and Kit's confused glares.

"How much do you love her, cowboy?" Selene asked.

"I'd take a silver bullet straight through the heart for her," RC said.

Selene glanced at Kit, then back at RC, taking a moment to find her brave, kick-ass side. "All right." This whole situation irked her. "Once I turn her, she's your problem. Understand?"

RC didn't say anything, he just stared at her.

She crossed her arms over her chest. "She's not coming back to life any quicker with you sitting there, eye-fucking me. Get out so I can do my job."

RC slowly stood and gave Charlee a kiss on the forehead.

"I'll come and get you when it's over."

RC nodded and she watched him make his way to the door. Kit stepped closer and she shot him a don't-you-fucking-dare-talk-to-me glare. If looks could kill, she'd just sent him deeper into hell.

Late the next day, Selene awoke to a moan. As she wiped the sleep from her eyes, her hand stung. Shit, she was still hooked up to Charlee. Ripping the needle from her arm, she stood and checked on Charlee. It had been twelve hours since she'd started the turning process and she was exhausted. She must have dozed off.

She despised this whole procedure. Every time she drained a human, a piece of her soul died. She understood the horror blondie would wake up to. The excruciating pain in her gut, the unquenchable thirst for blood. The sedative Selene had given her would take the edge off, and the O-positive blood dripping from the IV line should help control the initial bloodlust. But the girl was still facing hell.

Once the pain and cravings dulled, the realization would hit her cold and hard—she was no longer human, but vampire. A decision someone had made for her.

Selene felt Charlee's head for fever. It didn't surprise her that she had one. As soon as she was a hundred percent vampire, the fever would break. It was just her body reacting to the foreign substance invading her blood, fighting it like a virus. But there was no cure for her now.

Slowing her IV drip, Selene decided she was through baby vamp sitting. That was RC's job now. Once she was satisfied blondie was stable, she left the infirmary, dialing RC's cell.

He answered in one ring. "Yeah?"

"Tag, you're it. She's in recovery and will need your assistance once the sedation wears off."

"Selene?"

"What?"

"Thank you for saving my girl."

Selene hung up and shoved her cell in her back pocket as she walked down the hallway toward the elevator, then stepped inside. She needed a shot of whiskey. Okay, a bottle of Scotland's best would do the trick. It was still light out, so there was no going top side to the D&D. She tapped her foot impatiently, waiting for the big silver box to stop.

At the top level of the compound, Roman had converted an old room into a western themed saloon. She'd definitely find some whiskey there.

The elevator stopped and Selene stepped out. She hung a right down the hall, making her way to the saloon. She swung the double doors open. The springs creaked and echoed. The lights were off. "Thank Sweet Lilith," she sighed.

The whiskey bottles were beckoning her as she walked behind the bar and reached for a bottle of Highland Single Malt. She placed it on the bar while she hunted down a glass. Why she was hell bent on finding a glass was beyond her when she intended on emptying the damn thing. Perhaps after what she had just done to blondie she felt the need to be classy. She checked the drying shelf. "Aha." Two rows of crystal tumblers.

She poured herself a shot. Consuming it in one swallow, she slammed the glass down. She shook her head and squinted her face at the smoky aftertaste. The first shot was just a warm up.

She filled her glass again and then noticed the jukebox's lights glowing from the back wall. Hell, if she was drinking, she might as well get drunk with her friends. Emptying her glass, she poured another, then sauntered to the box. She flipped through the old forty-five records and made her country-girl-blues selection, starting with Johnny Cash's, "Ring of Fire".

She raised her glass to the first line of the song as it played. "You're telling me, Johnny."

She turned on her heels, dancing her way back to the bar stool where she'd spend the night sulking in the whiskey and listening to country singers belt out their sorrowful tales of lost love. At least she wouldn't be alone.

The song ended, and another forty-five flipped over, taking its place. Patsy Cline's rich, soulful voice sang out. She closed her eyes, taking in the lyrics and feeling their sting. She hummed along while her heart shattered into a million cold crystals. Goddess, with all the heartache in her life, she could write her own country song.

The swinging doors moaned open, breaking the moment—she wasn't alone. The air heated and a bead of sweat rolled down her spine. She could tell by the familiar way his boots hit the floor, who had walked in. There was only one man who could send a shiver through her body without saying a word.

"Pardon me, pretty lady, is this seat taken?" Kit drawled.

She motioned for him to sit. Probably a huge mistake on her part, being as she was half way towards drunk and numb.

Kit rested his elbows on the bar. "Look, I'm an asshole."

She raised a black brow. "Tell me something I don't know."

"Selene, I'm sorry—"

"Cowboy, I'm too drunk for all this sentimental bullshit. Don't kill my buzz."

"Fair enough."

A few moments passed in silence. Selene got up and went behind the bar. She returned with a tumbler, poured a drink, and placed it in front of him. "I hate drinking alone."

As he tilted his strong neck back, she watched him swallow the whiskey. His veins bulged underneath his skin, reminding her of how he tasted. Spicy-sweet. They had gone too far. She was never supposed to fall for her boss's son. If Roman knew the games they played, he'd have a shit fit and throw her out of the coven. But then again, if it was exciting and terrifying, why not pursue it?

Like a good hostess, she refilled his glass. With her drink in hand, she stood next to Kit, leaning her back against the bar. The record flipped again, and this time a song played about a man falling in love with a Mexican girl from El Paso. Another tragic love story.

"Dance with me, Cowboy." Selene turned around and set her whiskey on the bar.

She swung her hips seductively to the music, dancing toward the jukebox. She glanced over her shoulder and grinned at Kit as he glared at her with smoldering hunger in his eyes. She motioned for him to join her.

Kit downed his shot, licked his lips, and stood, never taking his eyes off her. Her heart raced. Goddess, the man had swagger. He could set her on fire without a single touch.

She teased him some more, swaying her arms over her head, playing the part of the wicked Lolita, casting her spell on the poor defenseless cowboy.

Kit wrapped his arm around her waist and pulled her close. Her breasts pressed against his chest; their bodies melted together. She looked deep into his eyes; this was no game. The sternness in his steel-gray eyes burrowed straight into her soul. She absorbed his strength, because, Goddess only knew, it was only a matter of time before she cracked and crumbled in his arms.

She laid her head on his shoulder and nuzzled his neck. She closed her eyes and breathed in that comforting spice and evergreen scent that was all Kit. *Why do you have to smell so good?*

With a soothing touch, he rubbed her neck, then ran his fingers through her hair. "Darlin'," he whispered.

The stubble on his chin raked across her ear, tingling her skin. She fought the urge to moan.

"Let me take care of you tonight."

Her body tensed. She knew exactly what he meant. By the end of the night, she'd be screaming his name, and in the morning hating herself for being so reckless. He'd leave her wrecked once again.

She lifted her head. And there is was...that pull. A connection she fought, yet she couldn't resist. "No strings attached?"

"No strings attached."

"Then take me home, Cowboy."

Chapter Sixteen

The wind blew in from an open window in her bedroom. She was back home at the ranch. The frigid air passed through her white sheer nightgown chilling her to the bone as she climbed out of bed, and padded across the room to shut the window. The curtains danced and snapped against the gust making it difficult for her to close the window.

She locked the window and turned back to go to bed, rubbing the cold from her arms, then froze. Something was moving. She squinted through the darkness to gain a better look; her eyes widened and her heart quickened when a man stepped out of the shadows, filling Charlee with a stampede of terror. *Mace?*

He reached out to her and his icy pull drew her in.

Mist permeated the air and clung to her body, and suddenly all fear was gone. Slowly, the weight of her troubles floated away like a balloon slipping from her hands and fading into the sky. Yet something deep within warned her not to let go of the string.

Charlee gazed into his dark depths searching for some clarity. Her mind fought against her body, telling herself to wake up, this was a dream, but her body ignored the demand and she stepped into Mace's wintry embrace.

She closed her eyes and laid her head on his chest as he wrapped his arms around her. The tighter he held her, the more her troubles disappeared as if he was absorbing them. Mace breathed her in. "There's no escaping me now, gorgeous."

Her eyes flew open and she took a step back.

A smile widened across his face. "Welcome to the family."

Charlee woke, thrashing her head from side to side, screaming no.

"Charlee?"

She opened her eyes and squinted against the brightness of the room. Everything around her was clearer, more vibrant. This wasn't a dream.

"It's too bright." She coughed through the dryness of her throat. It itched like she'd swallowed sand.

"Hold on, baby." The lights dimmed. "Is that better?"

She cracked one eye open, then the other. "RC? Is that you?"

"Yep, I'm right here." He held her hand.

She tried to sit up, but her head spun. What had happened? Like an old homemade movie flipping frame by frame, grainy bits and pieces were coming together. The smell of strawberries and vanilla, a knock at her door, duct taped to the driver's seat of a broken-down RV. The picture got worse. Mace's white fangs, blood pooling at her fingertip, the deed to her home. *Oh God, make it stop!*

150

An explosion, RC and her running for their lives, and then she'd blacked out. The images faded, leaving her stunned like she'd just watched a horror show and was left speechless at the shocking ending.

Her body ached to the bone. Even though the room was quiet, it was deafening. *Am I actually hearing RC's heartbeat?*

"What happened to me?" she asked.

RC stared at the floor. "I'm so sorry, Charlee girl."

"For what?"

"Do you remember the explosion?"

"Yes, I mean, I think so. Everything is still foggy."

"We didn't quite make it to the safe zone."

Charlee saw his face harden. This wasn't going to be good news.

"I failed. I didn't protect you. A piece of shrapnel pierced your stomach. You were bleeding out fast and..." RC stopped before he broke down.

"I'm no longer human, am I?" Charlee's voice quivered.

RC shook his head.

"I'm a..."

"Vampire. It was the only way I could save you."

"You turned me?"

"No, darlin', Selene did. I asked her to."

Her eyes widened. Charlee couldn't believe what she was hearing. It was too much to take in. Her breathing quickened. *Vampire?*

"Charlee, look at me." He squeezed her hand. "I'm going to make this right. I'm going to help you. I know I'm a selfish bastard, but I couldn't let you go. Not when we just found each other again. I hope you'll forgive me someday."

Charlee stared at the ceiling, paralyzed with confusion as a tear rolled down her cheek. How could he have allowed this to happen to her? He'd promised her protection, and he'd allowed her to become a monster.

An image of Mace flashed before her, sharp fangs and an evil smirk, staring at her, and she shivered. He'd gotten exactly what he wanted; the ranch and her soul. His essence flowed through her veins; she could feel him inside her and it shook her to the core.

"RC, you have no idea what you've done." She swallowed back the lump in her throat. Her mortal life was dead, yet her immortal existence would forever be tied to Mace. She was damned either way.

"It was the only way." RC hung his head.

"I want you to leave," she whispered.

Slowly, RC lifted his head and gazed at her like she'd lost her mind. "I'm not leaving you alone. You need me."

Something snapped inside her. She sprang up and pulled the IV from her arm. "I need you? Look what you've done to me." Charlee flew to her feet and stalked him, instinctively her fangs extended. "Get out!" She tossed the IV stand aside. "I don't ever want to see you again!"

RC grabbed her arms and tugged her against his body. His amber eyes glared into hers and she felt the intensity swirling behind them. "I'm going to ignore your last words, because I know you really don't mean it. Charlee, I'll give you some time to adjust, but don't think for one minute that this is over." RC released her arms and walked out the door.

"Fuck you!" Charlee screamed at the door as it shut. Finding the nearest thing to take her aggression out on, she tipped over a chair sitting in the corner. She whipped around and flung the bedside metal table over, shattering red-topped tubes on the floor. In a flash, she turned her fury to the hospital bed, tipping it over.

The shit-storm stopped when there was nothing left for her to destroy. Her chest heaved as she took in the room, shocked at the wreckage she'd left behind. Shocked that she now possessed such strength. She ran her fingers through her hair. Her heart shattered and she dropped to her knees, crying into her hands.

Time passed by, but how long Charlee didn't know. A blonde woman walked in the room, breaking her daze. "Charlee." She approached with caution. "I'm Thana." She knelt next to her and wrapped her arm around Charlee's shoulder, cloaking her in comfort.

Charlee leaned into the woman's embrace and broke down.

"Shhh." Thana stroked Charlee's hair. "If it helps, I understand what you're going through. I was robbed of my human life. I get it, you're pissed. But an immortal life isn't so bad."

Charlee sucked in a shaky breath. "He promised to protect me." She swatted at a tear.

"I know, sweetie," Thana reassured her. "Hey, let's get you out of here. You can stay with me."

Slowly, Thana helped Charlee to her feet.

Through a sleep fog, Charlee woke up in a dark bedroom, buried under a billowy blanket. She couldn't remember how she got here, too bad she couldn't say that about the nightmare that had just happened.

"Hey, sleepyhead." Thana walked in, holding two towels and clothes. "Thought you might want to shower when you're feeling up to it."

Charlee sat up and yawned. "A shower sounds amazing. Thank you."

"No problem." Thana smiled and laid the items on the bed. "I wasn't sure about your size but I think these will fit." She held up a pair of yoga pants.

"Looks like heaven to me." Charlee half-smiled.

"The bathroom is right there." She pointed behind her. "When you're done, we have some things to go over. Okay?"

"Sure." Charlee stepped out of bed and headed to the bathroom.

***

Charlee rinsed the dried blood off her stomach. She was surprised that neither a wound nor a scar remained from the wreckage. No, her wounds weren't on the surface, they ran soul deep. She glanced down her body, watching the suds run down her legs, revealing that her once tanned skin was now lighter. She flexed her calf and noticed the defined muscle. At least she still had her dancer's leg tone.

She shut off the water, grabbed a towel, and dried off. She slid the shower curtain open and froze. As she looked in the mirror her reflection stared back at her. She wringed her hair through her hands. "Holy shit." She could see her reflection. Well, that was one vampire myth debunked.

She stepped out of the shower mesmerized by the view. She turned her head from side to side, examining the changes. Her eyes were a more vibrant blue. Her cheekbones were more predominant. Awkwardly curious, she lifted her top lip and checked her canines. The ends were slightly sharper, but they weren't any longer. As she felt the tips a surge of emotions fled through her. Though she felt like the same woman as when she was human, the creature staring back at her was foreign. *Who am I and who will I become?*

Tearing herself away from the dreadful image, she walked out of the bathroom and over to the bed to dress. She slipped on a pair of gray yoga pants and a black tank-top Thana had lent her. A small striped case filled with toiletries sat on the vanity. Taking out a brush, she ran it through her hair and admired her new features. She had to admit…she was a beautiful monster.

***

A week had passed or maybe two, Charlee wasn't keeping track. She found herself slipping further into don't-give-a-fuck territory. She'd binge watched all seven seasons of Buffy the Vampire Slayer, until she was down to her last quart of ice cream. Yep, vampires liked the sweet stuff. Pushing up from the couch, she shuffled into the kitchen to throw out the double chocolate, killer brownie ice cream tub.

Her demons came alive at night, wreaking havoc. She'd paced the floors into the early morning, resisting the urge to feed. There was still a human side embedded in her that just couldn't allow her to drink another's blood. Call it morals, call it a death wish, she wasn't going there. Between sleep deprivation, being weak from not eating, and a certain cowboy waltzing in and out of her thoughts, she was exhausted.

Returning to the couch, she sat down in a huff, surfing the channels. Station after station and crap after crap. She shut the T.V. off and tossed the remote on the table. Her stomach tightened, a familiar sensation that was growing harder to avoid. She doubled over, breathing through the pain.

"Hungry, aren't ya?" Thana walked out of her bedroom fastening her hoop earrings.

"I'll be fine," Charlee bit out through clenched teeth.

Thana stepped in front of her with her hands on her hips. "You can't live off of ice cream alone. It's time you fed."

The pain dulled and Charlee relaxed into the couch. "I can't."

Thana sat down next to her. "Let me call a donor. Roman has several humans working for him who donate their blood. Once you eat you'll feel a lot better. Then Selene and I are taking you out."

"Wait...what? I'm not going anywhere."

Thana grabbed her cell from her back pocket and punched in a number on speed dial.

Charlee leaned over, looking over Thana's shoulder. "What are you doing?"

"Ordering take out." Thana winked.

"Please... no...I—" She reached for the phone, attempting to end the call.

Hi, Max." Thana swatted Charlee's hand away. "I need a favor."

What the hell was she doing?

"Can you stop by my place first?" Thana asked.

Her new self's needs outnumbered her human morals, and her heart pounded wildly at the idea that she'd finally feed and soothe the ache of hunger.

"Thanks, Max." Thana ended the call.

"You have about fifteen minutes before delivery." Thana stood and made her way into the kitchen. Charlee followed.

"What if I... you know, kill him by accident?" Charlee nervously asked.

Thana laughed. "You won't. Max is very good at what he does and has fed a few baby vamps. He'll take good care of you."

157

Charlee shook her head. "I don't know."

"Look sweetie, you gotta shit or get off the pot. You a vampire now, deal with it." Thana studied Charlee for a moment. "Have you looked in the mirror lately?"

Charlee did a look over at her baggy sweats and tee-shirt. "Guess it's been a while."

"Exactly. You're a stunning woman, Charlee, more so now that you're a vampire. Snap out of this funk and live your life. Sure you have a lot to learn, but you have friends who are willing to help. This isn't the time for foolish pride."

Something within those words hit home and Charlee saw where Thana was coming from. She needed to start living again.

"Once you've fed and get out of this room, you'll feel better."

"Fine, but where are we going?"

"Well, Val has reopened the D&D."

"Absolutely not," Charlee protested. "I used to work there. People would notice me and my—"

Thana stepped in front of her. "Sweetie, no one will ever know unless you tell them."

"But Val would want to know why I haven't been at work."

"Trust me, Val and Vin know what's going down," Thana snorted.

"Are you saying…?" Charlee cupped her mouth and her eyes widened.

"Not vampire, but demons."

"What?"

"You didn't know? D&D is home to a lot of dhampir and vampires. Well, I guess you wouldn't. They keep a low profile."

Shocked to the core that she'd been working in a vampire bar, and her boss and his brother were, she swallowed hard, demons, Charlee's new world just got real.

A knock at the door pulled her out of fucked up and crazy land. It had to be Max.

"Hey, darlin'." Thana kissed his cheek and invited him in. "This is my friend Charlee."

"Hi, Max." He offered his hand.

Charlee rubbed her sweaty palm down her pants before she shook his hand. "Nice to meet you." Maybe, maybe not. "So, um, where do we start?"

"Your bedroom if you want privacy or we can do it right here." Max pointed to the couch.

"No, my bedroom is right over there." She nodded across the room.

Charlee followed Max and paused at the threshold, hesitant to walk inside. *I don't know if I can do this.*

Max had removed his shirt and was ready to be bitten. Instantly, her eyes went to his throat, where a thick vein ran along the side of his neck. Her mouth watered, and she swallowed past the itchy grit.

"It's okay." He took her hand and moved her to the bed. "I'm a pro." He winked.

"I don't want to hurt you."

"You won't."

She wished she had that much confidence in herself, but she was terrified. She exhaled, her inner cheerleader shouted loud and clear, encouraging her to move forward.

She climbed in and lay on her side, facing Max as he lay down next to her.

"I'm all yours, baby." Max leaned back, resting his head on the pillow behind him.

Again her eyes went straight to his neck. She reached over and traced the pulsing lifeline down to his collarbone. It throbbed beneath her touch, and his skin was soft. A different scent mixed in with the air; he smelled so sweet. Acting on pure instinct, she leaned in and licked up the vein to his jawline. The old Charlee wouldn't stand for this. Hell, the old Charlee couldn't give anyone a lap dance.

Her stomach knotted as the first ping of pain hit her. She was famished and all she could think about was his blood. Her gums stiffened and she felt her canines descend. Her resolve broke and she nipped his neck.

"That's it, baby," Max moaned.

Her mouth widened and she clamped down on his neck. Blood ran across her tongue and she swallowed. As the hunger intensified, she fisted a handful of Max's hair and pushed his head further to the side, giving her more access to his vein. Not being able to control the flow, blood spilled from the corners of her mouth as she sucked harder.

A sudden high hit her veins, easing the pain in her gut. The strong sexual tension that went along with the bloodlust was building. She closed her eyes and all she could think about was RC. Him lying next to her. His neck she was drinking from. She pressed her body against Max's to ease the ache between her thighs. Her body was no longer hers as she surrendered to the animalistic need. "RC," she whispered against his neck.

"Whoa, let's take a breather," Max warned. "We don't want to go there. We just met."

Charlee's eyes shot open and she lifted her head. "I'm sorry." She wiped her mouth with the back of her hand.

"It's okay. Let's take five. Okay?"

Charlee quickly distanced herself from Max. "I think you should leave."

"It's perfectly natural to have those kinds of urges. Are you sure you want me to leave?"

"Yes. I'm fine now. I just can't go on." Charlee stood and handed Max his shirt. "Thank you for…you know…" She pointed at his neck.

"My pleasure." Max tugged his shirt over his head. "If you need me again, just call."

"I will." She smiled as she walked him out.

She shut the door behind him and walked over to the couch. She plopped down with her head in her hands.

How was she supposed to live a life without her cowboy? Her heart would ache for eternity.

Chapter Seventeen

RC cursed under his breath as he entered the D&D. "I knew you fuckers were up to somethin'."

Tibbs grabbed his shoulder and gave it a shake. "You would never have come if I'd told you where we were going."

And this was true. If RC wasn't on shift, he was sulking or drowning himself in the bottle. It dulled the pain in his chest, but did nothing for the hole embedded in his heart. He'd given Charlee the space she needed, and it was driving him mad. Charlee needed him, or did she?

RC thought that as soon as she'd cooled off, she'd come around and would have called. However, she hadn't. Three weeks and not a word. Was it really over?

Kit and RC shouldered their way through the crowd, Tibbs leading the way. "Hey, look who's here," Tibbs called over his shoulder to RC, and tipped his chin towards a table.

RC glanced over Tibbs' shoulder and saw three women sitting at the table, two blondes and a brunette. He didn't need to see her face; he felt her. *Charlee.* Their eyes locked from across the room, and suddenly time stood still. It was as if the crowd had disappeared and they were the only two left in the club. He couldn't breathe.

Charlee broke their stare first and looked down at her beer bottle, picking at the label.

As soon as RC could breathe again, his blood boiled. It wasn't by chance that they happen to be at the D&D at the same time.

"Asshole!" RC called out over the loud music. "You knew she was going to be here, didn't you?"

"Yep." In true Tibbs fashion he flashed his pearly whites.

"When are you going to butt out of my business?"

"When you stop being an ass," Tibbs said, "and go get your girl."

RC stood with his hands gripping his hips, avoiding the urge to haul off and punch him square in the jaw. He glared at Tibbs. "I'll be at the bar."

"RC—"

He held up his hand, shut the hell up understood. He turned and headed to the bar.

RC flagged down the bartender and ordered a double shot of whiskey. One drink and he was out of here. There was no need to stay any longer. He knew to leave when the party was over.

Seeing Charlee hurt like hell, yet he wasn't apologizing anytime soon for having Selene turn her. He'd stand firm on his decision with or without her approval. Yes, it was a selfish act. Yes, he knew better than to interfere with fate; however sometimes fate needed a kick in the ass.

The past few weeks he'd gone through the could have, should have, scenarios that tortured him, until he passed out drunk. But he couldn't wash away the truth that he'd failed her once again, and that alone was a burden he'd carry to the grave. *I should have stayed away.*

RC slammed his drink back, then reached into his back pocket for his wallet.

"So I see you were tricked too."

RC froze as Charlee's voice washed over him like a soothing balm. Hell, he'd missed her. "Yep," he said nonchalantly as he laid a twenty-dollar bill on the table, avoiding even a glance in her direction.

"Tibbs and Kit are over at the table. Come join us?" Charlee asked.

"Nah, just payin' for my drink. Then I'll be on my way." RC stuffed his wallet back into his pocket.

"Okay, I deserve the cold shoulder, cowboy. I said some hurtful words."

"Yep."

"I didn't mean it."

"Uh-huh." RC began to stand, but stopped as he felt her hand on his arm.

"Please look at me."

RC closed his eyes and inhaled; her magnolia scent was still there. His foolish pride told him to leave and make her hurt the same way she'd hurt him, but he couldn't. He sat down facing her, and looked into her blue eyes. He was defenseless.

165

"I'm sorry." Her voice shook. "Please forgive me."

RC took her head in his hands, rubbing her cheeks with his thumbs. "I was worried that I'd lost you, Charlee girl." He leaned in and kissed her lips lightly. "Can you forgive me?"

Charlee nodded. "We're even." She stood and wrapped her arms around his neck. He grabbed her ass, pulling her closer.

"I've missed you like crazy, girl." He nuzzled her neck.

Charlee took a step back, lustful eyes pinned to his. "V.I.P?"

"I thought Texas didn't do lap dances," he teased.

"Charlee does." She winked. "And I'm not talking about a lap dance."

RC hopped down from the bar stool. "Make up sex, great idea." He claimed her lips again. "You lead the way."

Charlee smiled up at him and caressed his face. "I love you, RC Reid."

He bent down and threw her over his shoulder, then took off toward the stairs leading to V.I.P.

"RC," she giggled. "I have two legs."

"I know but nothing is getting in the way of what I want to do to you." He swatted her ass.

As they made their way through the herds of dancing people, they passed the table where Thana, Tibbs, Selene and Kit were sitting.

Tibbs whistled out. "Ride em' cowboy."

RC shot back the one-finger salute.

Finally, they made it upstairs. RC rounded the corner to a long hallway where private booths with purple curtains for doors lined the wall. He took the nearest open curtain and went inside. He placed Charlee on her feet, claiming her lips. He trailed hot kisses down her neck and between her breasts, ripping the buttons off her shirt as he continued south. He tugged her bra straps from her shoulders, exposing her breasts, then he sucked a nipple into his mouth. He couldn't get her naked fast enough. There was no holding back this time. He dropped to his knees, kissing along her waist while working on her zipper. The thought of tasting her drove him crazy with desire. He peeled her jeans off and threw them aside. Next he stripped off her panties. He cupped her pussy and tenderly squeezed, still kissing his way down her body. When he couldn't reach any further, he hooked her leg over his shoulder and looked up at Charlee. He paused. If there was ever a moment to forever commit to memory, it was right now. The way Charlee looked at him rendered him speechless. The passion and love shone through those blue eyes of hers and it melted RC's heart.

"Hang on, baby." He winked and grinned.

Charlee held onto his head, threading her fingers through his hair as he dipped down and licked up between her folds, his tongue laving over her clit. One taste wasn't enough; he wanted to find out just how many licks it would take to make her shatter.

***

Charlee threw her head back. "RC," she moaned. Her legs threatened to buckle beneath RC's sweet torture. God, how she had missed him, missed this. He knew all the right moves that her body craved. He licked and sucked until she couldn't hold back any longer. A heatwave ignited her flesh and set her ablaze.

With her heightened senses since the change it didn't take long for her orgasm to hit. She gripped RC's hair, holding onto her balance as her body quivered, surrendering to RC's touch.

"I need you now," she panted.

RC stood and picked her up, and she wrapped her legs around his waist. "Fuck me," she whispered in his ear. She heard a growl and the next thing she knew she was up against the wall with RC unbuttoning his Wranglers. She nipped at his bottom lip before she sucked it into her mouth. Their tongues twirled with fiery passion. With a single tug, she ripped his shirt from his frame, sending snaps bouncing to the floor. Her body craved his touch, needing to feel every tantalizing inch of his body.

In one push, he thrusted deep inside. "You feel amazing."

He groaned and pumped faster.

Some kind of carnal impulse hit and her fangs descended. She raked them down his neck, wanting to bite him.

"Do it," he moaned.

Without hesitation she clamped down on his neck, puncturing his skin, and drank greedily as RC pumped her even faster. Her chest tightened and her body shuddered.

"Fuck yeah, Charlee girl. Come with me." He nuzzled her neck.

Lightning shot up her spine and she came harder than she'd ever come before.

She dug her nails into his back and screamed out her cowboy's name. A euphoric wave washed over her body as RC's cock jerked, releasing his seed deep inside her.

Charlee cradled his head between her breasts as RC stood catching his breath. They shared a different kind of connection now. He was soul-deep.

"I think we should fight more often," RC said, kissing her breasts. "Make-up sex is fucking incredible."

Charlee laughed. "As long as we make up fast. Three weeks was too long without you."

RC paused.

"What's wrong?" Charlee asked.

"You're right." He looked up and met her eyes. "Move in with me."

Charlee lost her breath. "With the Cowboys? I—"

"It will be fine, besides Hank misses you."

Charlee cupped his face. "I don't want to spend another second away from you."

"Then you're moving in?"

She nodded. "Yes."

169

Chapter Eighteen

Clay had been down in this dank dungeon one hour too long trying to convince the prisoner to come clean. His patience was wearing thin. The bastard had information that could help the Cowboys understand what the vampire king was conjuring up. Everything from the attack at D&D to Charlee's abduction, reeked of suspicion.

He rolled up his sleeves and wiped the sweat from his brow, then picked up a bucket. He unleashed the cold water over the asshole's face, causing his body to jerk back to life. Chains clanged together as the captive fought and screamed against the frigid chill.

When was he going to break?

Soon, he hoped. How much longer could his prisoner withstand being bound by silver and hanging from the ceiling by chains? Steam rose from his wrists and his upper body was weak from holding up his weight. His toes barely touched the ground.

Clay tugged his head back. "We know you're working for Mace Wrathmore. We've been on your trail since the attack at the club."

He grinned. "Bullshit. You know nothing."

"Do you call this bullshit?" Clay dug his finger into the prisoner's neck, retrieving a pill-shaped device. "That's a GPS tracking chip, asshole."

He hissed in pain. "You must be the bad cop. Where's the good one?"

"Unfortunately, it's your unlucky day. Are you going to talk now?"

"Seems to me you already have your answers."

Clay punched him in the face. "Don't smart off, son. I got all night, but by the looks of you, you're ready to break. I want to know why Mace has dhampirs working for him."

The captive swallowed, hard.

"You thought you could keep it hidden from me?" Clay grabbed his chin. "What does he want with Ms. Brysen's ranch?"

"Look, I was given a job to do. We were supposed to take out the stripper at the club."

"You mean Ms. Brysen?"

"Yeah. We didn't know y'all would be there. The bounty on your heads was extra credit."

Clay's jaw ticked.

"I don't know what he's going to do with the land. I'm just a worker bee trying to survive."

"I think you know, but can't tell. He's holding something over you, isn't he?"

The prisoner fell silent, sweat beading across his top lip.

The dhampir was young, eighteen at the most, and already corrupt. Dark skin encircled his eyes, his dark hair hair was greasy, and he was on the thin side. Clay's gut was telling him that he needed to help this young kid. Perhaps it was his own demons that were warring inside. Perhaps redemption lay within this young male. Whatever it may be, it was risky. Clay couldn't turn his back on him, because he knew firsthand how it felt to be down on your knees when the one person who you thought had your back was nowhere to be found.

Shit. When did I start giving a rat's ass?

"What's your name, son?"

"It doesn't matter," he mumbled. "I'm already dead." His head flopped forward.

"Hey." He tipped the male's head back and his eyes rolled back into his head. Clay slapped his face, trying to wake him. "Stay with me, son!" The prisoner's body convulsed.

Quickly, Clay freed him and flung him over his shoulder. Knowing that Selene was with Charlee, he decided to call Thana.

As he headed down a long hallway back to the elevators, he dug out his cell phone. "Come on, pick up." After a few rings he got her voice mail. "Shit." He was hoping she'd pick up so she could take care of the prisoner instead of him going to the emergency room above ground. Just his luck—he was headed to Diablo Medical.

Clay hit the parking garage, racing to his truck. He laid the dhampir down in the passenger seat, then reached into the glove compartment, taking out a long piece of rope, and secured his hands before he started the truck and left the garage.

What was he thinking? Had he lost his damn mind? Taking a dhampir to a human hospital ranked high on the bat-shit crazy list, but he had no other choice.

He followed the signs to the back of the hospital that led to a covered blue awning. He parked the truck, then raced over to the male, taking him into his arms.

Clay didn't bother to open the door, he kicked the damn thing open and rushed in like a thunderstorm, carrying his prisoner. "I need a doctor, now," he shouted at the woman sitting behind the reception desk.

"I'm Dr. Mason. What happened?" she asked as she bolted from the chair.

"I think it's a drug overdose."

"Let's go in here." She pointed to a room on the right and called for a nurse. "Lay him on the table." She took the stethoscope from around her neck. "His heart is racing." She checked the patient's body. "Why are his hands in restraints?"

Shit!

"For his own good." Clay untied him.

Clay waited for the prognosis while he checked the good doc out. Her hair was pulled back into a bun. The sorrel strands reminded him of his favorite ropin' horse. Eyes were full and green, and she had a body built for lovemaking. There was something about her that mesmerized his soul. It took a lot to stir his demons.

173

"One hundred nine temperature, doc," the nurse called out.

She removed her stethoscope. "We need to get his temperature down. Remove his clothes and cover him in cold towels." She opened his eyelids and shined her ophthalmoscope inside. "Pupils are dilated."

Clay stood back taking in the scene, praying that the kid would pull through.

"Let's give him some oxygen while you start an IV," she instructed the nurse. "Two liters to start and 30 milligrams of diazepam."

"Should I prep for gastric lavage?" the nurse asked.

"I want to get his temp down first."

"Right on it, doc."

"As for you…" She looked at Clay as she removed her latex medical gloves. "I have some questions for you."

Clay exhaled. This is when the bullshit story came into play. Hopefully, she'd buy it. However, she looked like a no nonsense woman.

"Let's step outside."

"Yes, ma'am." Clay opened the door for the good doctor, showcasing his southern charm.

As soon as they were alone, Dr. Mason wasted no time. "What relation is the patient to you?"

Clay removed his Stetson. "None. I was out minding my own business when I came across him. He approached me, asking for money, and that's when he had a seizure. I couldn't leave him on the street." Was that the best story he could come up with? Being this prick's cowboy hero, riding in to save the day. *Lame!* But for some reason, he felt the need to impress her. She wasn't buying it.

"So, you're just doing a good deed, Mr....."

"Holiday, Clay Holiday." He reached out to shake her hand, but the kind gesture was brushed off.

"So, we have no idea who this kid is then. Am I correct?"

"Correct."

"Well, Mr. Holiday..."

Almighty God, he loved the sound of his name coming out of her mouth.

"I think we're dealing with an Ecstasy overdose. High temp, dilated pupils, increased heart rate...I've seen my fair share of X overdoses."

Clay nodded, completely focused on her plump, pink lips.

"Once he's stable, we may need to pump his stomach, depending on the severity of his symptoms. I would also like to run some blood work to check for liver and kidney damage."

"All right," Clay agreed.

"Since we don't know anything about him, and you're not related, you're free to go."

"Nah, I'll stay. I want to make sure the kid has someone here when he wakes up."

And there it was. He finally got a smile.

"Ok. It might take a while, though."

"Sure. You go tend to the boy. I'll be in the waiting room."

Clay watched as she turned to go back into the room. Before she entered, she glanced over at him. "There's coffee on the third floor."

Clay tipped his head and smiled.

He wanted to wait so the kid didn't wake up alone? Again, he called bullshit. The boy was still his prisoner and the only link the Cowboys had to Mace.

Hellfire! He knew darn well that the kid was on drugs, he could smell it. But it wasn't Ecstasy. Dhampirs could tolerate large doses of human-made drugs. The same amount that could kill a mortal did nothing for half-breeds. Unless... Clay stopped mid-stride. Unless Mace was drugging young dhampirs.

Damnation!

As he stepped outside to move his truck, he called Roman. This wasn't good for the Cowboys. The sole purpose of the brotherhood was to protect their race. It was what they fought and died for. How could their own blood turn against them? This drug had to be some powerful shit.

"Hey, Roman. We need to talk."

Chapter Nineteen

Two weeks later

RC slammed the door closed to his truck. He revved the engine to life, then sped down the highway. All damn day his mind had been busy on his girl and he couldn't wait to get back to the compound. He loved the feeling of coming home after his shift topside, knowing she'd be waiting for him, especially when she met him at the door wearing nothing but her pink cowgirl boots the way she'd done the day before. He'd barely had time to hang his rope before she dragged him back into the bedroom to have her way with him. He loved every minute of it. Life was going well for them.

RC looked down at his belt—he was an official Hell's Cowboy now. It had only been a week since they'd held a special ceremony to induct him into the brotherhood. Roman stood proud while he handed him the signature buckle. The silver skull was prized more than any other buckle he'd won during his bull riding career. This one held a new purpose. He'd found a family with the Cowboys and Charlee.

But there was another reason he was busting at the seams. The white envelope in his front pocket. He had a huge surprise for Charlee and couldn't wait to tell her.

"Hey." Tibbs grabbed his attention.

RC glanced at him. "What?"

"What's with the grin? You've been smiling like a fool all day."

"Can't I be happy?"

Tibbs sulked. "I reckon with a female like Charlee waiting for you back home, I'd be grinning like an idiot too."

RC fixed his eyes on the road. There was something bothering Tibbs since they'd left this morning for work. It wasn't like him to be a Debby Downer. "Hey, if it bothers you to have Charlee and Hank at the compound, we can move to another room. I have no problem asking Roman."

"Nah." Tibbs waved him off. "I'd miss her cooking too much."

"She does keep us well fed." RC smiled. "So what's wrong, man? You're sulking."

Tibbs adjusted his seat so he faced RC. "I don't know. Maybe for once, I'd like to have a woman to come home to."

RC about hit the brakes. Tibbs settling down—no way. He'd seen the cowboy in action, giving the ladies his hillbilly special. His thirst for sex was unquenchable. One woman would never be enough.

"I'm tired of all the meaningless sex. I want more. You know, like what you and Charlee have."

"Well, first you have to stop fucking around," RC said sarcastically

"Do you think I like being this way? I have no choice, it's what *he* wants." Tibbs shook his head. "I'm fucking cursed."

RC was taken aback by the hostile tone in the cowboy's voice. "What do you mean what *he* wants?"

"You'd never understand."

"Probably not, but there has to be a woman out there who'll put up with your shit."

"Let's just change the subject." Tibbs faced the window, staring out at the desert.

Yeah, there was definitely something brewing in that head of his; RC could feel the tension radiating off him.

The rest of the ride was spent in silence.

Once inside the compound, RC strode down the hallway heading to his room. He opened the door and was surprised that Charlee wasn't there to greet him. Hank ran to him, jumping on his legs. "Hey boy." He greeted Hank with a tummy scratch.

"Honey, I'm home," he called out as he hung his hat and rope by the front door. He tamped down the panic when Charlee didn't respond. She was probably playing some kinky game, lying naked in bed.

He raced to his bedroom and swung the door wide. Nope, no Charlee. Perhaps she was in the tub. *Oh hell yeah, a bubble bath.* He rounded the corner into the bathroom. The door was open and there was no sign of her. "Charlee, no more games. Where are you, girl?"

RC ran back to the living area and knocked on Clay's door. "Hey, have you seen Charlee?"

No answer.

Next, he knocked on Kit's door. No one was home.

Running his fingers through his hair, he turned around, his eyes searching the compound as he thought about where she could have gone. The sun had set…then it dawned on him—the ranch.

Grabbing his hat and rope, RC ran like a bat out of hell to the parking garage.

***

Charlee walked up the stairs to the bedroom she'd occupied since she was a kid. For the last week she'd been wanting to come home and pack a few things before Mace took possession of the property. The heartache was eating her alive. She'd spent the last two weeks trying to convince herself to come, but she couldn't take the pain of knowing she'd failed to keep her family's ranch. RC had warned her that it was too dangerous for her to go alone, but what he didn't understand was that she had to say goodbye on her own.

A tear rolled down her cheek as she set the box down on the bed. The sheets were still a wadded mess from the last time she'd made love with RC. She picked up a pillow and held it against her face. God, it still had her cowboy's scent all over it.

Shaking her melancholic daze, she made her way to her dresser and packed a few pieces of jewelry Gran had given her, a pink teddy bear, and some old pictures hanging from the mirror. She quickly rummaged through her drawers. Tears welled in her eyes and her hands began to shake. Perhaps it was too soon to come back home.

She sniffed back the tears and walked over to her closet and flipped through the hangers. Each garment characterized who she used to be. In frustration, she tore the clothes off the hangers and threw them on the floor. She felt like an imposter.

This room represented a different life—a girl who had been much simpler compared to now. A life she longed to live again. She mourned her former self.

She looked around the room; this was a bad idea. She had to get out of here. Grabbing the box, she headed down the stairs and stopped when she reached the bottom step. Pictures from the fireplace mantle beckoned her. She sat the box down on the couch. One by one, she dusted off the old picture frames, then laid them in the container. Even though she was no longer the country girl from next door, she'd never forget where she came from. These treasures were all she had left.

The front door busted open and startled her. RC rushed in. "Charlee, you had me worried sick." He hugged her tightly.

"I'm sorry. I didn't mean to scare you." Stepping out of his embrace, she wiped her wet cheeks with the back of her hand.

His big strong hands framed her face. His eyes darkened with worry. "What's wrong? And don't tell me nothing."

"I needed to come home."

"Darlin', we've talked about this. I was going to bring you here."

"I know, but this is something I needed to do on my own."

"Charlie, you can't just go topside by yourself. It's too dangerous."

And there he was, coddling her like she was helpless. Since she'd turned, he'd been shielding her from danger, things that didn't even exist. She wasn't allowed to leave the compound unless he was with her. Some days, it felt like she couldn't breathe. She needed her own space and purpose in this new life.

She took a step back. "For the past two weeks I've been cooped up in your bedroom. I've waited like a puppy for you to come home day after day. I'm not allowed to go anywhere on my own. I feel like a caged bird, RC. I have new wings and I need to fly and explore."

She waited for his response. He stood with his hands on his hips, his jaw tight.

"You can't protect me all the time."

"Don't you think I know that? Hell, Charlee, it kills me that I couldn't save you." He pinned her with a hard glare. "I did whatever it took to keep you, and I'd do it all over again if it meant you staying in my life. I can't live without you." His voice cracked.

She watched him walk out the front door.

That didn't go well at all. Looking up, she exhaled, calming her frazzled nerves. All she was asking for was space. Time to figure this shit out.

Charlee walked outside and onto the front porch, where RC was sitting on the swing. Her heart dropped as soon as their eyes met.

"I'm sorry. What I was trying to say didn't come out like I wanted it to."

RC reclined in the swing and motioned for her to sit down next to him. He wrapped his arm around her and she nuzzled against his warmth. "I had dreams before all of this happened. And now I've lost them all."

"Not all. I have something in my pocket for you."

"Oh, you do?" Charlee raised a brow.

RC reached into his front shirt pocket and pulled out a white envelope, then handed it to her.

"What's this?"

"Open it."

Peeling open the envelope, she took out the tri-folded paper and began reading. Her mouth dropped open. "Are you serious?"

RC smiled. "Yep."

"You bought me a bakery?"

"Well, it needs a little elbow grease, but the building is solid and spacious. I thought we could whip it into shape, together. I know it's not the ranch, but—"

"I can't believe it." A tear slid down her cheek.

RC turned and faced her, concerned. "Baby, I didn't mean to make you cry."

She shook her head. "RC, you've made my dream come true." She wrapped her arms around his neck. "Thank you."

"I'd give you the world if you wanted it."

Charlee slid back and gave him a suspicious glare. "This building wouldn't happen to be located in the area you patrol. Would it?"

RC scratched the back of his neck, avoiding her question.

"Good, because I expect you to come by and see me on break. I'll make sure I have those strawberry cupcakes you like."

RC slid his hand behind her neck and pulled her close. "I love you, Charlee Brysen. I'll make this work for us."

"No, we'll make it work, together." She claimed his lips, kissing him passionately.

Even though she'd been through hell and back, her life felt complete. She had her cowboy, with extra benefits, forever, a bakery, and a new life.

A chill snaked down her spine. She wished her skin pricked for RC, but the twinge was pure evil. He'd always be there, hunting her through the shadows.

Chapter Twenty

Mace watched from his limo as the happy couple kissed under the moonlight. It wouldn't be long before Charlee would feel his wicked presence, which was exactly what he wanted, to strike fear, forever making her look over her shoulder wondering when he'd come for her. The problem was he grew impatient. That one taste of her lingered on his tongue and left him craving more.

He pulled out his cell phone and punched in a number. It was time to settle a long overdue score. Did she really think he'd forget about her and what she'd done to him?

"Yeah."

Years had passed and her voice was still as smooth as silk, enticing like a fine wine, and sunk in straight to his soul.

"Selene."

There was a pause. He heard her suck in a deep breath and hold it.

"How did you get my number?" Selene asked.

"It doesn't matter. You knew I would find you eventually."

"Mace, I'm in no mood for bullshit. What do you want?"

"Did you really think I wouldn't find out?"

"I don't know what you're talking about."

"The girl you turned. Ms. Brysen?"

There was silence.

"I wanted to thank you for that. I regret not turning her myself. She's divine."

"You leave her out of this. It's me you want and I won't allow Charlee to become one of your pawns. I made her. She's mine."

Mace laughed. "She's yours? Well, I'm sitting in my limo right outside her ranch. She's with her cowboy. It's a shame I'll have to crash the party. She's coming home with me tonight."

"Bullshit."

"Have you forgotten? My blood runs through your veins; the same blood now runs through hers. You knew I would find her. Maybe you wanted me to find you. Is that true?"

"Fuck you!"

"Aw, love, it's time you came home."

"I should have put a bullet in your heart when I had a chance to."

"Regrets are a bitch." Mace ended the call with satisfaction. He'd gotten under her skin. *Now the fun begins.* He smirked.

Mace opened the car door and silently made his way to the front porch where Charlee and RC were sitting on the swing. He clapped his hands, congratulating the couple. "Bravo, I've always loved a happy ending."

RC bolted from the swing, sneering at Mace. Before RC could make a wrong move, Charlee stopped him by grabbing his arm. "What do you want?" RC seethed.

Looking surprised, Mace held his hand over his chest. "Ms. Brysen, you haven't told your cowboy the news."

RC looked at Charlee. "What is this asshole talking about?"

"RC, I should have told you sooner, but I couldn't."

"Tell me what?"

"Oh, this is good, really good." Mace grinned.

Charlee glared at him and his cock hardened. He couldn't wait to get his icy hands on her.

"RC—" Charlee began to tell him, but their attention was drawn to the front yard as Selene materialized.

She approached Mace and his breath caught in his chest as she stood in front of him with her hands on her hips. "Selene."

There was an awkward silence.

"Will somebody please tell me what the hell is going on?" RC called out.

"RC," Selene drawled. "Meet my maker."

"What the…?" RC stepped down off the porch and approached Selene and Mace. "That means this asshole will forever be tied to Charlee."

"RC, calm down and take Charlee home. And don't you dare be mad at her about this. I'll take care of it."

"We're not leaving here without you," Charlee said as she joined RC.

Selene shot her a glare. "Leave now. I command it."

RC and Charlee reluctantly walked to his truck and left.

"As for you," Selene tipped her chin to Mace. "I want you to leave that girl alone."

Mace took a step closer until he could feel her breath on his skin. "I'll leave her alone on one condition. Leave Roman and his half-breed fuck-ups and come home to me." He ran his finger down Selene's neck, feeling her swallow. "Because I'm such a nice guy, I'll give you time to think about my offer." He grabbed her chin. "Don't make me wait long."

He walked back to his limo, adjusting his suit jacket. He loved playing these cat and mouse games. In the end he'd get what he wanted; he always did.

Book Blurb:

Will you be ready to serve when Hell's Cowboys come for you?

There's a new sheriff in town. With his coven torn apart by corruption, vampire Roman McCoy leads a posse deep underground to prepare for the battle of their lives. His newest recruit, cowboy RC Reid dies after a bull ride and awakens to a new world with vampire benefits. He now could be the key to taking down the vampire king of Diablo, Texas. Torn between the fanged advantages of his new life and the memories of his old one, there's one thing RC can't leave behind, Charlee.

Charlee Brysen lost everything the day a bull killed the only man she'll ever love. But that's not the only thing that vanished, so did her dreams for college. Now she's about to lose her family ranch and will do anything to save it. Stripping for cash, her life is flipped upside down when RC waltzes into her club and demands a lap dance. Besides being dead, there's another little problem; he has fangs!

As the King of Diablo tightens his icy grip on the coven, Charlee's life hangs in the balance. RC must save her, but will their love be stronger than blood?

About the Author

Victoria Zak is an international best-selling author of the Scottish Historical Paranormal Romance series the Guardians of Scotland. Her first book Highland Burn, was a 2015 RONE award finalist for best paranormal romance. She has also written in the World of DeWolfe Pack, Amazon Kindle Worlds, for USA Today best-selling author Kathryn Le Veque.

When not conjuring her next story, Victoria enjoys spending time with her husband and two kids.

Victoria loves to hear from her readers. You can connect with her through the links below:

Website www.victoriazakromance.com

@VictoriaZak2

https://www.facebook.com/VictoriaZakAuthor

My Immortal Cowboy

Books by Victoria Zak

Guardians of Scotland Series:

Highland Burn

Highland Storm

Highland Fate

Highland Destiny

Hell's Cowboys Series

My Immortal Cowboy

Kiss Me Deadly (2017)

Hell on My Heels (2017)

Stand Alones

Once Upon a Winter Solstice

De Wolfe's Honor

The Jewel of Grim Fortress